Further praise for

American Son

"In bare and muscular prose, *American Son* deftly seduces with this emotional yet unsentimental coming-of-age journey. Enter the unnerving world of Gabe and his cultural swirl of barrio attack dogs and Hollywood high-rollers, backwater California truckstops and the devoted Filipina mother he is ashamed of. Roley opens a window to an Asian America that is rarely acknowledged and perhaps even unrecognizable; his is the searingly honest voice of an authentic American son."

—Helen Zia, author of *Asian American Dreams*

"Reads like an emotional live wire. Roley's terse, raw prose gets right to the point, leaving no questions unanswered about the pain that can be inflicted between family and the crushing confusion of immigrant identity. . . . One of the most stunningly affecting and original works in the past few years. . . . A frightening and unapologetic look at both the immigrant and bi-racial experience, introducing us to a cast of original characters who have been brought to life with prose so sharp it hurts." —Neela Banerjee, *AsianWeek*

"Penetrating. . . . Roley explores this omnipresent yet usually invisible story of contemporary American immigrant life with an easy exactitude and a dry, unmerciful eye. . . . Clean, beautifully understated prose."

—Suzy Hansen, *Salon.com*

"Hard-hitting and brash, this debut novel takes a cold, clear-eyed look at the American immigrant experience. . . .

This is a powerhouse story of vulnerable strangers in a brutal, alien land told with stylish restraint, bare-knuckled realism and tender yet tough clarity."   —*Publishers Weekly*

"Roley's sparse minimalism renders masterfully the moral desert in which Gabe and Tomas exist. . . . Roley . . . captures the angst of young boyhood memorably and ably, set against backgrounds of lyrical beauty."
                    —Vince Gotera, *North American Review*

"Roley never judges his characters but rather shows the pain and anger that propel their actions. His clipped and poetic style serves the novel well, and readers will be compelled to follow this tale to its violent and ambiguous conclusion."   —Brendan Dowling, *Booklist*

"Gabe's narrative succeeds in displaying the kind of cultural isolation that breeds anger, turning a smart, quiet boy into an avenging victim despite his wish to do the right thing. . . . A new voice to watch."   —*Kirkus Reviews*

AMERICAN SON

A Novel

Brian Ascalon Roley

 W. W. Norton & Company · New York · London

To my parents,

Thomas and Azucena,

and my sister,

Carla, and Gwen

Copyright © 2001 by Brian Ascalon Roley

Printed in the United States of America
First Edition

For information about permisson to reproduce selections from this book,
write to Permissions, W. W. Norton & Company, Inc.,
500 Fifth Avenue, New York, NY 10110

Manufacturing by Courier Westford
Book design by Dana Sloan
Photograph for interior design by Stephen Shore

Library of Congress Cataloging-in-Publication Data

Roley, Brian Ascalon.
American son : a novel / Brian Ascalon Roley.
p. cm.
ISBN-13: 978-0-393-32154-8
ISBN-10: 0-393-32154-1
1. Filipino Americans—Fiction. 2. Mothers and sons—Fiction.
3. California—Fiction. 4. Immigrants—Fiction. 5. Young men—Fiction.
6. Gangsters—Fiction. 7. Brothers—Fiction. I. Title.

PS3568.05333 A84 2001
813'.6—dc21   00-053307

W. W. Norton & Company, Inc.
500 Fifth Avenue, New York, N.Y. 10110
www.wwnorton.com

W. W. Norton & Company Ltd.
Castle House, 75/76 Wells Street, London W1T 3QT

5 6 7 8 9 0

Contents

AMERICAN
SON

PART
ONE

Dear Ika,

I am thankful for your letter of March 15th. We appreciate your prayers, and you and your sons will of course be included in our prayers as well. Here in Manila things have been busy. Julita will soon be graduating Ateneo, and we have been renovating the house in preparation for her graduation party. Some of our walls are for the moment no longer standing and last night a typhoon rain battered the plastic tarp the workers had put in place for protection. You can imagine my surprise when I awoke this morning to find the living room flooded! I am certain the weather must be nicer for you in Los Angeles.

It is with concern that I read of your boys' declining studies. Perhaps Gabe's biology grade can be dismissed as an aberration—one which must be punished, of course—yet the case of his older brother appears most serious. It came as a surprise to me that Tomas was expelled from Saint Dominic's, particularly given that he is accused by Father Ryan of committing violent behaviors. I still recall Tomas as the quiet and handsome boy who visited us here in Manila as a child. With his American father's blood he has the mestizo looks of an actor. No doubt if you had remained in Manila, as I had warned you to, he would have fared well and you would not now have so many worries. Here Tomas would have known what it means to be a Laurel, its responsibilities and expectations. In fact, if he had shown any delinquent propensities I would have certainly spoken severely with him myself, and made communications with his teachers. My circumstances and connections have improved since you left the Philippines, and I believe that I could have averted his expulsion.

In fact, I suspect that in writing me you may have hoped that I could communicate with his American teacher, Father Ryan, as he had formerly served as a chaplain here in Forbes Park. I will try, yet as I have no other connections in Los Angeles, I am not hopeful in this regard. I can only advise you to attempt to gain admission for Tomas into another Catholic school, a stricter one if that is possible in a place like California.

Also, you must be careful whom you let him befriend. I find it particularly puzzling that a Filipino boy such as Tomas should choose to spend his time with poor Mexican children when there certainly must be nice American and Asian children of successful people in Los Angeles.

May I suggest that you consider bringing Tomas and Gabe here to Forbes Park for a visit? I know that you do not like to take my money for plane tickets you cannot afford, but we would be most pleased if you were to change your mind.

We will be praying for you and your sons always.

Love,
Your brother Betino

Balikbayan

South Santa Monica,
California
April 1993

Chapter one

I

Tomas is the son who helps pay the mortgage by selling attack dogs to rich people and celebrities. He is the son who keeps our mother up late with worry. He is the son who causes her embarrassment by showing up at family parties with his muscles covered in gangster tattoos and his head shaved down to stubble and his eyes bloodshot from pot. He is really half white, half Filipino but dresses like a Mexican, and it troubles our mother that he does this. She cannot understand why if he wants to be something he is not he does not at least try to look white. He is also the son who says that if any girlfriend criticized our mother or treated her wrong he would knock the bitch across the house.

I am the son who is quiet and no trouble, and I help our mother with chores around the house.

The client is some man from the movie business who is coming over any minute so that Tomas can help him train the dog he bought to protect his home. This morning I have been helping my brother wash and train his dogs, which he calls "guard dogs" to the people he sells them to, but which you should really call *attack dogs* since we use methods he learned from cop friends he knows on the LAPD. Each time I come to the cage, they clamber against the rusted wire, throwing themselves against the links and barking for my attention. All week I have been replacing the old wood boards, rotted and nearly broken from the dogs' thrown weight. Despite my efforts, the wood bends and threatens to buckle and snap under their weight. The door pushes outward as if the cage has inhaled a great amount of breath. I unlatch its aluminum bolt, then let it come open a few inches—and stop it with my shoe. The dogs nudge at the stopped door. My hand slips inside and meets their wet noses and warm fur and the warm wet feeling of their tongues and drool.

Cut it out, I tell them.

They do not listen to me. They are far too excited, though if I were to use a German word—one my brother uses to train them to attack—they would become instantly attentive.

Quiet.

I find the one I want, Heinrich, and grab his collar and tug him out between the other dogs. They look disappointed, and some even wail. I give Greta and Johan and Sigmund quick pets and hush them, then shut and relatch the cage. They bark at my back, though they soon realize I am not going to let them out and they settle down. It is all I can do to keep hold of Heinrich's collar as I lead him across knee-deep grass to the training area. He ignores my shushing until I finally get impatient and tell him to quit it in German. *Las das sein!* He immediately quiets and stands at attention, ears perked. Though it is easier this way—and he follows me obediently now—I prefer not to use these commands since he changes from an affectionate pet to an alert and serious guard dog. He becomes all duty.

We find my brother at the shed, pulling out the burlap and plastic armor which he wraps around his arms for protection.

Tomas looks up at us. The sunlight makes his pale scalp, shaved like a Mexican gangster's, glow through his black, three-day-old stubble.

What took you so long?

The dogs all wanted to get out.

They always want to get out.

I look down. Sorry.

He turns to the dog. Heinrich stands stiffly, pressed against my leg. His ears prick as he looks at Tomas.

Don't look so excited to see me, Heinrich.

As Heinrich senses that Tomas does not yet need him to be alert, the dog's muscles relax and he pulls away from me—his fur sliding gently along my jeans—and he hurries to my brother. Tomas reaches over and hugs him and scratches behind Heinrich's ear. The tattoo on the back of my brother's neck—a black rose whose stem is wrapped by vinelike barbed wire—emerges from beneath his stretched T-shirt collar. He always wears a sleeveless T-shirt so people can see the tattoos along his muscled arms. The tattoos are mostly gang, Spanish, and old-lady Catholic. As he leans forward, the thin fabric of his shirt moves over his Virgin of Guadalupe tattoo that covers his back from his neck down to his pants. She wears a black robe and has deep, olive eyes. Crushed beneath her feet are the Devil's horns.

My brother is bent over, tongue-kissing Heinrich.

Good boy.

He looks up from Heinrich and regards me. You better wash him. The client's coming soon.

I did wash him. I washed all the dogs.

He doesn't smell like it.

You know I did, Tomas. You saw me.

Well then maybe you'd better do a better job.

I grit my jaw. You shouldn't complain. It's not like you pay me.

Fine, he says. Don't help if you don't want to. Sit inside and watch TV all day for all I care.

He turns away, letting Heinrich trot after him. I do not want to follow him, but I do not want to go back into the house either. Finally I do come alongside the house, batting aside the overgrown old trellis vines, and emerge onto the front yard. My brother sits on the porch. He is waiting for the client, the dog scrambling around on the threadbare grass before him, chasing a worn tennis ball Tomas threw onto the street. With sunlight coming through dusty overhanging branches, the street resembles an ocean bottom beneath a sunny kelp bed.

I linger at the lawn's edge. He ignores me for a while, then calls out, Why you standing all the way over there?

I keep my mouth closed and my arms crossed.

Stop sulking.

I'm not sulking.

Sit down. If the client sees you standing there like that he's gonna think you're my houseboy.

This is a lie, of course, but my face goes hot, which is what he was after. I do not want to sit after what he has just said, so I stand there for a moment. But I feel foolish, so I walk past him and enter the front door, to see if our mother needs any help inside.

II

All morning our mother has been cleaning up the kitchen so she can look out the window as Tomas prepares Heinrich for the client's arrival. I know it is hard for our mother to imagine the quiet boy he used to be. Right now Tomas is playing around with a false canvas arm. The dog leaps on it viciously, shaking it like a white shark thrashing a tenderloin on a harpoon, and on each impact she flinches. The client finally arrives around noon. He is a screenwriter or a producer or something. Mom studies this man who wears ratty black jeans meant to make him look casual, polished wing-tip shoes, and a maroon silk shirt. He nervously eyes the dog that will soon go home with him.

Who's this man, Gabe? she says to me without turning from the window. Her finger touches the glass.

I don't know. Some producer or something.

Hmmm, she says suspiciously. Does he own a nice mansion?

I wouldn't know.

She wipes the countertop she has already cleaned three times, her finger still bearing her wedding ring even though my father left us a few years ago and Tomas and the relatives think she should not wear it. She touches her earlobe and sighs. Well, I don't see why such a man needs a dog to guard his house. He's not such a big celebrity. Who does he think he is?

Maybe he's married to one.

Of course not. You tell your brother to come in before your aunt arrives and sees this dog attacking him.

The first time the client arrived he asked why my brother named the dog Heinrich. Tomas always gives the dogs German names and trains them with foreign words. He tells the celebrities and rich people he sells them to that they have pedigrees that go back to Germany, and that they descend from dogs the Nazis used. He likes to tell them Nazi scientists did experiments in dog breeding just as they did in genetics and rocketry. He tells them this is a Teutonic art that goes back to the Prussian war states. All this is a lie, of course. But the clients seem to like the explanation, even this movie producer who has a Jewish name. He paid six thousand dollars for the one dog and it was not even the best in the litter.

The celebrities also like that Tomas wears tattoos that tell you he belongs to the Eighteenth Street Gang. Tomas is six-three and you can see the definition of his muscles through his shirt. Sometimes he takes his shirt off. Not too many young white people have a huge tattoo of the Virgin Mary on their back and a gold crucifix dangling from a chain against their chest. He never tells his clients he is not Mexican. Sometimes he buys pit bulls in Venice or downtown where all the black people have them chained in their alleys and when you drive through the alleyways you can hear them barking for miles. The sound echoes between the buildings. He can buy them for forty dollars there and then place an ad in a West LA newspaper like the *Evening Outlook* and sell them for a couple hundred dollars. Sometimes he gets them from Compton or East LA, but he never lets me go with him anywhere east of Crenshaw. They are cheap nasty dogs and not even the best guard dogs, but ever since they started killing children everyone seems to want one. Selling them is an easy way to get money; Brentwood and Santa Monica people will come with cash (our neighborhood is at the poor end of Santa Monica, bordering Venice, so it does not scare them) and they do not expect the pit bulls to be trained. You do not buy one to be a nice pet, or a safe one. You chain them to a tree outside your house and dare people to attempt to get inside. A lot of young white people from West LA come because they want to be cool and think owning one is like having a tattoo or being branded on a shoulder or arm. But celebrities do not buy pit bulls. They buy American bulldogs and Rottweilers and Tervurens and Bouviers and other expensive dogs that require extensive training. Purebreds. My brother used to sell Akitas, but after Nicole Simpson's dog failed her, people on the Westside stopped buying them.

Mainly Tomas prefers to breed American bulldogs—pedigrees—and he raises them and trains them and he pets them and sometimes he even has to feed the puppies from a bottle. The ones he keeps long enough he trains according to the Schutzhund method. Each time he sells a puppy he falls quiet and pretends he does not care about it leaving, that he will never see it again. He will not scratch its chin or pet it in front of a customer, but afterwards, he will go to the window and watch the customer carrying it down the steps. Sometimes he will stand there for a very long time.

The client—Rosenthal—stands at one end of the backyard as he waits nervously for Tomas to fasten on his protective armor. The dog sits patiently now, wagging his tail. Tomas walks twenty yards across the grass and turns and nods. The man calls out a word in German and the dog sprints across the yard, barking viciously, and leaps at my brother and grabs his arm. I know it hurts even with the armor on. Sometimes you get bruises that trace the shape of a jaw. The dog will hang there on your arm, like a pendulum, until the client calls out for it to stop in German. Sometimes the clients get so mixed up and nervous they forget the word. Tomas cannot say it because he is being attacked and the dog is trained not to listen to him. Once a dog missed my brother's arm and caught him in the stomach, but fortunately I was there and called out *Aus* and the dog let go and sat down obediently, wagging its tail. It had love in its eyes again, longing for my brother's attention. Spittle still dripped down its gums and neck.

III

After our father left us, our mother started calling up her brother—Uncle Betino, who lives in the Philippines—for advice on how to deal with me and Tomas. They soon got into a dispute, however, over some jewelry and old statues of the Virgin Mary their mother owned before she died. Our mother had long, distressed conversations on the telephone, and Tomas (still small then) would hover nearby while she was on the line. Sometimes she would sob. Other times she simply wrapped a strand of hair around her finger. Mostly she worried about an old piece of jewelry, a silver pendant which had been with the family for over a century and had come to Manila on a ship from Spain. Grandma had added her own diamonds to it, and meant for it to pass down to our mother. But Uncle Betino was in control of the estate and decided to give it to his wife Millie, who had hated

Grandma and treated her badly on her deathbed. For that reason our mother didn't want her to have it.

Tomas did not talk much then, and he would stand in the hallway most of the time so she would not know he was listening, though afterwards—after our mother calmed down—he told her not to give in to our uncle. He asked if she could get a lawyer, and she said it was the Philippines and you could not sue for something like that there from a man like our uncle. He lived there, he knew people, and anyway had more money than we did. Tomas thought there must be something she could do, but she would get so upset he would finally drop it. I knew he was mad by the way he moved around the house doing chores or building model rockets. Uncle Betino came to Los Angeles a year later and he took us out to dinner. Even though he and our mother had argued about the pendant on the phone, now they acted warm with each other, the way Filipinos have to even when they are angry, and our mother and Millie kissed cheeks in greeting. I shook our uncle's hand. It was dark and callused and firm. He touched the side of my shoulder as though he were going to slap it, but then gripped it warmly and looked into my eyes. It was all I could do not to lower them. It was hard to imagine him making our mother cry. After he let go, he looked around to greet Tomas. But my brother wasn't there.

Our mother found him in his bedroom, shades drawn. She made him come out but Tomas did not look into Uncle Betino's eyes and shook his hand loosely, though after feeling how hard our uncle's grip was, Tomas suddenly started clenching his hand harder. Uncle Betino's face changed and he squeezed down tighter. My brother winced, though he tried to hide it. Uncle Betino was very nice to Tomas the rest of the night. He ordered him extra spare rib appetizers. He addressed him often, though he made sure not to ask him questions Tomas could refuse to answer. In this way, my brother could just sit there quietly and not be rude. He did not say anything during that dinner, but Uncle Betino did not lose face, and neither did our mother.

That night Tomas stole our uncle's wallet but Mom found out and made him return it, and she told our uncle that Tomas had found it on the floor and was merely safeguarding it. Our uncle was not fooled, but he took it back smiling and thanked him.

Afterwards, Tomas would not do any chores around the house and barely talked to her for a week. He sat in his room watching TV and refused to do any homework, which is how he knew he could most hurt her. Two years later, our father returned from his station in Germany and Mom took him back in. On his third night home he got drunk and started smashing my model rockets and I tried to tell him to stop and he struck me. Mom tried to make him stop and it looked as if he would hit her too, but then Tomas came out of his room. He was larger than our father now. Dad stood over her making fun of Filipinos and her family and looked as if he was about to hit her, and my brother dragged him outside and tossed him onto the acorn-covered lawn. Our father picked himself up and stumbled towards his car, then leaned against the hood. He wiped his forehead and then looked up at my brother—Mom and I saw this from the front steps—and told him he only married her because he wanted someone meek and obedient, but had been fooled because she came with a nagging extended family. He said he never intended to come back to us permanently anyway and only wanted to sleep with her, and now he had gotten what he wanted and would leave and did not care if we wanted him back or not. I doubt he really meant the worst of what he said—there was, I remember, hurt in his voice—but Tomas came up to him and shoved a fist into his side and then slammed his head into the window. After our mother drove him to the emergency room, we never saw him again.

IV

Today, Heinrich is pretty well trained—the man has been here four times already—and the dog always catches Tomas below the elbow. You have to know how to take it or you could dislocate a shoulder. Our mother pretends not to notice each time the dog leaps at my brother and digs teeth into his arm, but I always catch her staring out the window. She had not wanted him doing this, but Tomas finally managed to assure her it was safe. She relies on him to tell her how things work in America, and it has become easy for him to convince her of things. Now she likes the dogs as much as Tomas and me—in particular, Tomas's favorite breeding dog, Buster, the only one he did not give a German name since he refuses to sell her. She is a bitch, but he named her the masculine Buster because he had always wanted to name a dog Buster. Since Tomas often does not come home at night, our mother feeds Buster and so Buster no longer sleeps with Tomas but goes into her room and curls up at the end of her futon. At first she complained about the dog's smell and hair in the sheets. She still does complain, but actually she has become used to Buster's company.

Sometimes at night I will pass by her bedroom on the way to the bathroom and if the moon is out you can see Buster curled up at the edge of our mother's bed, on the sheet's wrinkled shadows; or at times even on the small edge of mattress by our mother's pillow, her hind leg hanging over the futon edge. Sometimes our mother has a hand on Buster's neck, as if she were her husband. It seems strange that our mother would like Buster so much considering what the dog did to Saint Elmo and Sister Teresa. Saint Elmo was our mother's white cat, who was sweet: everyone liked him because he would go up to strangers and rub his head against their legs, and his gums against their shoes. She called the girl cat Sister Teresa after some Spanish nun who founded the Carmelites, Mom's religious order. This cat was skittish and shiny black and liked to hide behind the couch. Saint Elmo and Sister Teresa got along with the dog all right if a person was around. But one day I came home and Buster had Saint Elmo in her mouth; the cat was still crying. Buster wagged her tail as she looked up at me, all proud, and was surprised when I kicked her and tried to get the cat out of her mouth. But it was too late.

Mom loved Teresa best of all because she was weak and skittish and afraid of things. At night our mother is afraid of the wind in the trees. She will not admit she is afraid of ghosts, but when the Santa Ana winds blow, she turns on all the lights and puts on the TV and then vacuums the house. The vacuum and lights drive Tomas crazy. He teases her, tells her she is acting like a maid fresh from Manila. Tita Dina says our mother is afraid their dead father will come back.

Why are you afraid of your dad? Tomas once asked her.

Outside the hot wind rattled branches against the house.

I'm not. She looked embarrassed and turned away from Tomas and focused on her dishes.

So why you turn on the TV and shit? You hate TV.

I don't know, she said. I don't like the sound of the wind.

So you're afraid.

No.

Was Grandma afraid he'd come back?

She paused. She did not look at him although he was close behind her.

Yes, she admitted.

He shook his head. You would think you'd want to see your relatives again, he said.

She hesitated. She looked flustered and probably thought she should not respond. Finally, she did. But he's dead.

Wouldn't you want to see me come back if I was hit by a car? he said. What about Gabe? He said this glancing over at me with an expression meant to imply I was a mama's boy.

Our mother did not like to think about this. She turned off the faucet and walked into the living room. Tomas followed her. So you wouldn't want me to come back? he said.

Come on, Tomas.

I'm offended.

No you're not.

I am, he said. My own mother.

You're just saying that.

You wouldn't want me to come back, he shook his head.

Maybe because Sister Teresa was careful she lasted longer than Saint Elmo. Although Saint Elmo had occasionally bullied Sister Teresa, they usually got along and often curled up on the couch by the back window and he licked her face while she licked at his leg. After he died she would sit there alone, only occasionally jumping down to try to get you to lick her head like Saint Elmo had. After Saint Elmo died I could not get the sound of his cry out of my head, or the image of his panicked look in Buster's mouth. I wanted to give Sister Teresa away to our cousin Matt, but my mother and Tomas wanted her around. She lasted about four more weeks.

Now when the winds roar outside on hot Santa Ana nights, rustling through the dry brittle leaves and branches, on nights when your hair feels staticy against your pillow and your legs sparkle beneath the sheets in the dark while the window rattles in its pane, Mom has a special pork biscuit to entice Buster away from the windows. The dog thinks she hears animals and prowlers out there, her nose pressed to the glass, though it is only branches clattering in the trees. If our mother feeds her enough, Buster sleeps on her bed and keeps her company.

V

She has gotten used to seeing the dogs throw themselves at Tomas in front of clients. But today she is especially nervous because she expects Tita Dina and my cousin Matt for lunch. She has already patted on her makeup and used curlers to make her hair ends curl off her face, as though she were going to work. She imagines Tita Dina might think she is not the best mother.

She turns off the faucet and comes up to me where I am sitting at the Formica counter reading a magazine. Gabe, she says.

Yeah?

When will your brother be finished with this man?

I don't know.

Will it be in an hour?

I don't know.

She looks at me. Will you ask him?

Why don't you ask him? I say. I do not like to nag my brother because you never know how he might respond. Also, it was my brother's idea to invite them over in the first place. He wants to ask our cousin Matt if he knows any movie people who might want to buy dogs. Matt went to a private high school founded by Episcopalian hippies. He teaches there now, and movie people pay a lot of money to send their kids there. Our mother does not know I am worried about annoying Tomas, and she looks at me as though I were lazy and ungrateful.

It's just one little favor I'm asking.

Okay, I'll do it.

Just one little favor.

I said I would do it, Mom.

She stands there and shakes her head.

Okay.

Lately she has begun talking about moving back to the Philippines to grow old, because she has no husband to take care of her and American children put their mothers in nursing homes. We tell her we will not, but she says American wives would not have an old Asian lady living with them. Tomas says he would smack any bitch who treated her badly. Still, our mother likes to run down a list of cousins and nephews and other distant relatives who live in the Philippines and she wonders out loud whether she should call up and ask for a visit.

Right now she probably does not want to go outside, because Tomas would not want the client to see her. Also, movie types and other important people make her self-conscious about her accent. Sometimes she has me come with her to do errands so I can do the talking for her; I do not mind so long as we go someplace like the DMV, where I am unlikely to run into someone from school. At my school—Saint Dominic's—everyone thought I was white, for a while. Tomas had gone there first and he had passed as a white surfer. There were no other surfers there, but he was known as one—he even bought a board and had our mother take him to the beach three times a week—and he put Sun-In in his hair, though instead of turning blond it went all red. Then he began hanging out with Mexicans, who are tougher. He stopped surfing and dyed his hair black again. If anyone tried calling him an Asian he beat them up, and he started taunting these Korean kids who could barely speak English. Father Ryan brought him in to talk about it, to see a school psychologist. And he hated it when Tomas started wearing a big gold cross; that was what Mexican gangsters wore then. Each time my brother taunted a Korean kid Father Ryan would call our mother in to pick Tomas up, and it embarrassed her. She would lower her head and apologize, saying she was a bad mother, so finally Father Ryan had to reassure her. It angered him that Tomas made her feel ashamed. In the classroom Father Ryan called on Tomas and ridiculed his answers and made pointed comments about the way he dressed and looked. Finally, Tomas got kicked out of school for smashing a Japanese boy's car window with a tire iron. By then people had figured out I am part Filipino. Still, I do not like having her pick me up from school. She is short and dark and wears funny-looking giant purple glasses that are trendy on other people's mothers but which do not match her brown skin tone.

I emerge into the brilliant backyard, the sun on my face, while behind me the aluminum screen door clatters into its loose frame. The producer appears to be the sort of man who takes walks on Montana Avenue upright and confident, even when he passes skinny models, though today he does not look too confident. Seeing me, he acts uncertain, as if I were important and not just a fifteen-year-old brother, probably wondering if he should tell Tomas I'm here.

My brother can hear me approaching, but he takes a few drags on his cigarette before turning around. You can see the Virgin through his shirt back, the Devil's horns beneath her feet.

He turns to me. What you want?

How long are you gonna be?

As long as it takes, he says.

Tomas has not told the producer what to do with the armor he is holding, and the man awkwardly watches us, waiting to be told what to do with it. He has a bald spot I never noticed before, but in the sun you can see his pale scalp glowing through his dark thinning hair. You gonna be an hour? I say.

I don't know.

Mom wants to know.

He hesitates, giving me a look that says this is none of my business. He shrugs and says maybe an hour.

I go in and tell this to our mother.

An hour?

Yeah.

She looks at the clock. It is half past noon. From outside a German word comes through the window and then the sound of Heinrich barking.

Why? I say.

They're supposed to be here at one.

She pretends she is worried about having Tomas free to

greet Tita Dina, though really she does not want her sister to see this dog attacking Tomas in our backyard.

You want me to tell him to finish up? I ask.

No, she says, returning to her dishes with trembling hands.

VI

After our father left us, Uncle Betino kept trying to get our mother to bring us back to Manila so we would be disciplined and educated and Asian, but she did not want to leave America.

Nowadays she threatens to return to the Philippines because American wives will not take care of their mothers-in-law, but the last time we went there our mother did not seem to miss the country all that much. She complained about the heat and smelly showers, even the ones in Uncle Betino's Forbes Park mansion. Relatives took us on trips to Palawan, Quezon, Visaya, and other islands, and when we checked into the hotels each night she unpacked clean sheets she'd brought from America and made us fold them over and sleep in them. She pushed the beds away from the wall so insects would not crawl onto the sheets. She warned us not to eat unpackaged food from local stores, and washed her hands after touching shopkeepers at the markets. In the evenings, when we returned to the room, she threw herself on the chair and sighed.

Manila smells like cockroaches, she said, and scrunched up her nose.

Why are you so tired? Tomas said. He was sitting on a bed, reading a book by James Michener.

It's hot.

But you grew up here, he said. You should be used to it.

Well I'm not, Tomas. She was plucking off her damp stockings, reluctant to do this in front of us.

Take a shower.

The bathroom's dirty.

Didn't you have dirty bathrooms when you were a kid?

I've lived in the States longer than the Philippines, she said firmly. I'm American now.

You don't talk like it.

She frowned. Anyway, mostly I'm tired from dealing with all these relatives and their dramas and gossips. This country's crazy.

Don't you like seeing them? You were laughing a lot over lunch.

They can be funny, that's true, she said, and a smile came to her face. But I would hate to live here again. Everything's about appearances. They're all afraid of being poor, so they act like they're rich, and talk tsismis about each other behind their backs.

We're poor back home, he said. Here we'd be rich.

She shook her head. No, Tomas. You should appreciate America. I went there so you could be an American.

Thanks a lot, he said.

That was several years ago. Last August an aunt invited us to visit her farm in Palawan, said she would pay the plane ticket. Tomas and I wanted to go. We remembered the dark river caves filled with blind chirping swallows, and their miles of ceilings lined with sleeping red-eyed bats. The maids who brought you Cokes and drivers who waited for you outside of malls. But our mother shook her head to Tita Adorie even though she was on the telephone.

No, she insisted.

I could tell the aunt was persisting, asking why, and though our mother could not give her a good explanation, I remembered our last trip there and how melancholy she had seemed.

VII

The client comes out the side buttoning his shirtsleeve at his wrist and smoothing his hair flat. In the shade of the avocado tree you cannot tell his hair is thinning. A few more sessions, and he will be able to take his dog home. He appears to be thinking and not paying attention and he does not see me sitting on the edge of the porch until he is almost upon me. Startled, he halts suddenly and there is a moment of fear in his eyes and then he recognizes that it is only me and they calm again.

Hey, he says.

I nod.

Earlier he seemed afraid of me, around the dogs and Tomas, but now that his eyes are calm I have to focus on his chin so it will look like I am holding eye contact. He appears to be waiting for me to say something, but I cannot think of anything, and he continues on and leaves.

Chapter two

I

Today Tomas has to deliver a dog to a celebrity in Brentwood Park. I have not been to a celebrity's house before, and this morning I woke early and waited for him to get up so I could help. He walks into the kitchen and fixes a bowl of cereal without saying a word. Though yesterday he told me I could come, he does not normally take me on these trips, and I wonder if I should ask him again to make sure. But he looks too touchy to be bothered. Finally he finishes eating. There is still sleep in his face as we go out back and as he swings the wire door off the cage. I reach in and retrieve Johan, the best of the pups, who pants with an energy that comes from being young, though he is large already and fully trained. Tomas goes in and grabs Buster—Johan's mother—and drags her onto the grass. She stays close by him, making anxious circles.

Cut it out, Buster, he says, looking down on her. What you so worked up about?

She must sense we're gonna sell her son.

No shit.

No shit, I say. If it's so no shit then why'd you ask her why she's so excited.

I'm just making talk with her, Junior.

He turns away to rub her under her chin reassuringly, pressing his cheek down against the back of her neck. She whimpers and rubs her side against him like a cat, then sits down on her haunches again.

Are you gonna sell Buster, too? I say.

What do you think?

No.

Without a word for me, he rubs her fur to shake off bits of dirt and dried-up leaves. Then why'd you bring her out? I say.

He pats Buster's side seriously and lets his hand rest there. It's the last time she'll get to see her son. I want her to see him to the last.

We take the dogs through the house—Johan for the last time—and it seems to me a shame that our mother is not home to see him off. They seem to sense something is wrong, and they quicken their pant. Johan breaks free and scrapes across the kitchen linoleum towards the far end where, when he was a pup and allowed to live inside, we used to put out his dog dish. He sniffs in the corner, confused, and even shoves his nose up against the wall at the memory of where he used to push the dish against it.

Tomas hollers. Johan looks up, ears perked, and comes dutifully back.

In the meantime, Buster has wandered into and out of our mother's room, where she still sleeps, as if today might be the last time *she* would smell it.

Tomas lets the dogs into the car first, and they climb in back. Their fear—if they ever had any—has transformed into excitement, and as they peer out at me their breath fogs the windows. Their noses leave moist dots on the glass.

Tomas gets inside. As I reach for my door he leans over and locks it.

The handle does not move. What you doing? Open the door.

You aren't coming.

Don't be stupid, I say. Let me in.

You deaf?

I try the handle harder again, though it will not budge. The dogs have their claws clambering against the glass, watching me. Tomas looks forward, inserting the key and revving the engine.

He pretends to be warming up the car, though he is waiting for me to plead.

Come on, Tomas, I finally say. Let me come with you.

He turns to me and rolls the window down a crack.

Why should I?

I want to see this celebrity's house.

He looks me up and down and shakes his head.

One look at you and they'll think these dogs were raised by a bunch of wimps.

I look aside and do not answer him, pretending to stare off at the neighbor's cactus plant. Nails scraping against the glass sound like keys clicking.

The door snaps open.

When I turn to him, he throws some of his clothes and junk off the seat onto the floor.

All right, you don't have to cry, he says. Come on in.

I do not move. I'm not crying, I say.

I'm not going to ask you again, he says. So you can come along and look at the house or stay behind.

Without a word I get in and we pull out and the car humps over the lump in the asphalt, a great warp above a tree root, and the dogs fall against my seat back and I can hear their eager panting.

We pass beneath the 405 overpass, entering its shadows, and above us I can see patches of sky between the bellies of the freeways that appear blindingly bright and blue, and the sun flickers over the dogs' faces until we come out into the daylight again. The dogs watch the sun, then the wetbacks who stand in golden shafts amid the shadows waiting to get picked up for work, short little men who smoke cigarettes and talk in groups.

Here the dogs peer at the buildings we pass: the mix of discount stores West LA people come down to shop in; taquería stands for the wetbacks who live three or four families to an apartment close by; a Starbucks on the way to the on-ramp that looks posh once you get beyond the iron railings that protect it.

I wonder if the dogs can see our reflections in the rapidly passing glass, in mirrored and tinted storefronts. In these reflections I can make out Tomas, me, and the dogs—just barely—and it looks as though they are looking at me, but I doubt they can see anything. They cannot even see the images on a television screen.

II

We stop at the Brentwood Country Mart and have the cheese pizzas we used to come for with our mother each time we visited our Tita Dina, who lives close by. It is strange how they have this covered courtyard with benches surrounding a tree; it feels somehow rustic, even though we are in the middle of a great urban city, and the people who frequent it are rich and mostly Jewish, from Brentwood Park. Daylight floods in pleasantly and we have always loved sitting here, but it seems sad without our mother this time. Tomas buys the pieces and folds mine over like a taco for me, the New York way our father showed us, then he gets some fries from the chicken stand and brings out the little cups of barbecue sauce they have that we always loved to dip them in, and he shakes the garlic salt seasoning on.

Dig in, he says, and folds his own piece over.

A few people watch us eat. Probably they are taking note of Tomas. A fortyish woman in slender black bicycle pants and a pink T-shirt. An older woman I recognize who works at the toy store. The wetback behind the pizza counter who spoke a few words of Spanish to my brother. Tomas did not understand the Spanish, though he nodded and tried to make it look as if he understood. I wonder if Tomas senses all this attention as he hunches over his piece. Probably he does, though he pretends not to, or at least not to care. In those days when we came with our mother or aunt nobody ever paid any attention to us, except at the toy store where they knew us, or the market where we bought chocolates, and the bookstore where Tomas used to read magazines and talk to the old skinny man who ran it and smelled like shoe polish and who would recommend to him all the Michener books my brother loved because they would take you to far-away places. Even after he stopped reading them, I would scour his old copies and buy the latest books. The same skinny old man still works there; he looks the same, but didn't recognize us walking in. He watched Tomas carefully as he paused to look over a few magazines and then told him not to look unless he was going to buy one. Tomas crumpled the one he was reading back into its slot and made his way to order our pizza.

Tomas buys a couple of drumsticks for the dogs and lets me feed them once we get into the car. As we roll up Twenty-sixth Street you can see the Santa Monica Mountains up ahead. Their sadly wrinkled sides face south, sunbathed in worn shades of purple and blue. My fingers are covered with slobber and sticky, plum-colored barbecue sauce that does not come fully off onto a napkin. We pull off San Vincente, and immediately it is as if we are in the countryside. There are mailboxes here, on the streets. There are no sidewalks. On some blocks you can see huge lawns leading to houses that look like they belong in the countryside or on some farm, but on other blocks the houses are barely visible, surrounded by fences and trees and gates with intercoms and video cameras.

This is a cool neighborhood, I say. It's just like being out in the countryside.

Tomas ignores me. He concentrates on the road. From the way his tendons rise on the back of his hand, gripping the wheel, I can see how tense he is, though he tries not to show it. Probably it is his car which makes him nervous, a white Oldsmobile, the type Mexican gangsters prefer because they can pile so many people into the backseat. He studies the houses and gates and fences and intercoms, the mani-cured lawns and cobblestone driveways. Strangely there are no cars parked on the curbs here; they are parked beyond the gates in the driveways, Mercedes, BMWs, and some util-ity vehicles too. The dogs circle about the backseat, worry in their eyes. It could be they have picked up my anxiety, or maybe they sense that something will soon happen to change their lives forever.

Look for the address, Tomas says.

I can't make them out, I say. None of them have numbers on the curbs and you can't see past the fences into the houses.

Sometimes we pass iron gates, and I get a glimpse of a house and then only trees and fences again.

I tell him to slow down.

He looks at me, the amused asshole grin of this morning on his face again. You nervous or something?

No. I just can't read the numbers.

You can't read numbers? A lot of good it does you to bury your face in those books you read.

I could read them if you'd slow down.

We round a corner and enter a canopy of tree branches that tunnel above us like interlaced fingers—between its knuckled branches, the sun is nervous and flickering. The lawns appear brighter from this shade.

Just cool down and relax, Junior. I cleaned out the car in case we get pulled over.

I told you, I say. I just can't read them.

Often in this car we get pulled over, and sometimes the cops make us get out and put our hands on the warm hood and they frisk us. They run their hands over our back and sides and along our inner thighs. Tomas complains about it at family dinners and says they are perverts and racists, but Tita Dina tells him he is getting what comes to him for dressing like a Mexican and driving a hoodlum car.

Finally we get to a white brick house that has narrow columns, fronted by a circular drive. I can see all this through the gate, which is wrought iron, unlike those of the neighbors' houses. Through a window above the front doors I make out that this house has a three-story entryway, and an enormous chandelier of dangling glass hangs from the ceiling.

This is it, I say after spotting the numbers above the

country mailbox. As we pull up closer I can see it is aluminum, with a little red metal flag.

Dang, he says. That's some kind of a house.

I don't know. I think I'd like mine to be closed in like the neighbors'.

You mean you want it to be all fenced up and hidden?

Sure.

Why? he says. You afraid some photographers are gonna try and take your picture?

I do not answer him.

His eyes stay on me, then he looks forward and grins. I wouldn't count on it, Junior, he says. You'd have to be pretty famous for somebody to want to take a picture of a person with a face like yours.

Mom has said he should not tease me like this, but I do not remind him. I look out my window.

He continues observing me, carefully.

What you looking at so intently, Junior? he says. Haven't you ever seen a bush before?

There is a white rosebush before me which I have not noticed until now. But I do not look away from it.

I got news for you, Gabe. Celebrity bushes are the same as the ones owned by you and me.

You don't own anything, I tell him. Only Mom owns bushes. You have to have a job to afford a house.

I make plenty with the dogs and stolen stereos.

That's not a real job. It doesn't count.

Okay, Mr. Stockbroker, he says as we pull up to the gate. He stops and lowers his window before a white intercom perched on a metal stand. Tomas pushes a red button. We wait. He tries again and after a minute a lady's voice that sounds Mexican—probably the maid—asks what we want.

We've come to sell some dogs, he says into the box.

Again, the sound of static. Then the crackled voice comes on and says they don't take solicitors.

No, listen, Tomas says. We have the dogs with us now.

We no take solicitations, it says.

Then the static clicks off.

Tomas frowns and hits the side of the intercom and presses the button. I already talked to the señor of the casa, he says to the voice when it comes on again.

You speak to him already?

Sí.

There is a pause, and then the voice says *okay* and the gate slowly swings open. Its iron bottom scrapes along the driveway. You'd think they'd get a faster motor if they can afford a house like this, he says.

That was really great Spanish, Tomas, I say.

Fuck you, he says.

III

We pull up behind a black Land Cruiser that sits high on extra-tread snow tires, and in the polished paint a sunny, ghostlike reflection of our white car warps and twists as it nears. The dogs are nervous, thumping against my seat back.

Tomas pops open his door and gets out, pulling Johan after him.

Should I bring Buster out too? I say. She looks at me, then at Tomas—confused—and then to Johan, before laying the side of her head against my bare forearm.

No.

But don't you want her to see Johan off? I thought that was the whole point.

It is, he says.

I pause.

So?

So Buster *is* coming to see us off, but I didn't say anything about you coming inside, he says.

I am silent.

I don't want you coming in and fucking it up, he says.

He tells Johan to sit and the dog does, then my brother pulls the seat up again and Buster scrambles out. By now Johan has gotten excited again, and I hear his panting all the way from the passenger seat. His head turns back and forth as he looks rapidly around, making half circles like a cat. Buster comes up beside him, and he looks at her quickly, almost nudging her, but moves away again, distractedly, as he takes in his new surroundings.

I'm not gonna fuck it up, I say.

You'd fuck it up just looking the way you do.

What does that mean?

I mean take a good look at those clothes you're wearing. One look at that and they'll take the offer back for sure.

I don't think they'd care what I wear, I say, and come out of the car and force myself to hold my words. I want to ask him why he is being such an asshole, and when will he get over it, but I am beginning to wonder if he has actually become one. My eyes tear and the sun blinds me. If I cried maybe he would stop, but to prevent this from happening I stare hard at the house, studying it. Through the glass in the front double doors a brown-skinned woman approaches. She wears cheap jeans and a faded red T-shirt, probably a maid. She opens the door and steps outside.

She stands on the brick porch, a hand on her hip, regarding us suspiciously. No doubt she has heard some of our arguing. Tomas composes his face into his hardened unreadable expression.

He leans over and whispers to me, not turning or looking me in the eye. Calm down. And behave yourself if you think you can.

I *am* calm.

You can come in if you want, but don't say a word, he says. And don't stand too close to me or the client.

He mumbles something to himself about it not being hard for me to not say a word and then turns his back to me and climbs halfway up the porch towards the maid. She studies him—probably wondering if he is a real Mexican, or what other hot country he might have come from—glancing once towards me, then back to Tomas again. He has worn his thin T-shirt again so the white client can see the Virgin of Guadalupe through it. In front of her he seems embarrassed, though, and he keeps it turned away.

I grab Buster's collar and whisper for her to be quiet. She stops whimpering.

The lady sets her hands on her hips and regards her. She makes a lot of noise, the woman says.

It's not the one you're going to get.

She looks at Tomas as if surprised to hear his voice. This noise, it sounds like this one is not very happy.

Tomas nods seriously. She's the mother.

It takes a moment for the gears in the woman's mind to put it together and then I see the understanding pass behind her eyes.

Oh, she says, and nods her head. This one is the mother. I see.

We wanted her to say goodbye, he explains.

She nods and comes up to me—no longer suspicious—

and reaches down and clenches the fur at the back of Buster's neck, then starts squeezing in a way meant to be rubbing. The woman is so close to my face now I can smell her hair spray.

Yes, she says. It is hard for a mother to see her child go.

She regards me as if for the first time.

Hello.

I mumble a greeting after I lower my eyes. Still, I can feel her smiling as she studies me. My face turns red.

She turns over her shoulder to Tomas, not letting go of Buster's neck. Ustedes son hermanos?

He looks like he doesn't understand but doesn't want her to know this.

She wants to know if we're brothers, I tell him.

I know that.

He glares at me and I shut up, but she faces me now and expects an answer.

Sí.

Yo creo que no.

I nod. Mi madre tampoco lo cree.

She bites her lip and thinks a moment.

Se parecen por la forma de sus ojos, she says, and then turns to Tomas: You do not seem so. But I can tell it in the shape of your eyes.

When he catches me looking at him he glares at me, and I look down. Even with the woman still rubbing her neck, Buster manages to rub her side against my jeans, and keeps pressed there, whimpering. The woman notices this.

This is your dog? she says to me.

I shake my head. No. It's my brother's. And my mom's.

She smiles. But she goes to you when she knows her son will be leaving.

She's only a dog, I say, then look down again. She can't know he's going.

The woman smiles. A mother knows.

She lets go of Buster's neck, then reaches over again to scratch behind her ear—a last time—then starts up the stairs, leading us inside. Tomas goes first and I hesitate in the doorway, not knowing if he wants me to go in, but the maid turns to me and makes several rapid friendly waves for me to enter—as if I were silly for thinking otherwise.

I duck my head and follow.

IV

Most people wonder what sorts of homes celebrities live in, probably picturing something modern: white carpets and trendy furniture, marble gourmet kitchens, a view onto an exercise room with chrome equipment. But we find our celebrity in a dark room with wood-paneled walls and an old pool table with lions carved on its legs. Tomas runs a finger over the green cloth, and I do too. It is felt-less and bare as silk. The table has no pockets. The man comes up to us, pulling his robe string tighter, and looks out the French doors at the canyon view. At its bottom rests a golf course covered with brilliant sand traps shaped like oval moons. There are hills and valleys of sunny grass surrounded by mansions. I knew none of this was here. The drapes are held back by gold ropes, their braidlike tassels dangling.

He turns back to us and I see that he does not have the mustache he has on the TV show. His hair is thinner—the shiny scalp shows through the blown-dry strands—and his skin is far tanner, almost leathery beneath his eyes. But his eyes are as alive and young as the cop character he plays. He studies us sharply.

So you've brought the dog, he says. He has some sort of a southern or western accent, which surprises me since in the movies he always talks like a blue-collar cop from New York City.

Yeah, Tomas says.

The man shakes his head. But there's two. I don't remember asking for two.

This one's the mother, Tomas says. It's her pup you're going to get.

The man studies the dogs. He scratches their heads with his thick fingers, like a man who has been around animals, not like the urban detective he normally plays. He does not seem a bit afraid of them. He returns to Buster and sets his cheek against her ear and scratches firmly under her neck.

This is a nice one.

Tomas nods.

A lovely animal, the man says.

She's got good genes. Johan has them too.

The man purses his lips and nods to himself thoughtfully. He's a good dog, he agrees. He returns to Buster and she comes up and sets her side against him. But this one's better.

Tomas leans a hip against the pool table.

Johan is younger.

The mother's friendly.

Johan is too, my brother adds. He's just nervous now.

The man sets his cue stick on the carpet, gripping it upright like a staff, and his thumb rubs the tip. His thumb comes off, covered by green chalk. He looks firmly at my brother. Look. I grew up on a farm in Georgia. We had dogs like this one—American bulldogs. They're great guard dogs, but they aren't German. So don't try conning me about animals.

The man's thumb stops moving, very still on the tip, and his face is pushed close to my brother's, and though I can tell this bothers Tomas, he tries not to show it, and he does not lean back.

I'm not trying to con you, mister.

Just because I live in Brentwood doesn't mean I haven't been around the block. We used to hunt with hounds. Big yellow-eyed beasts. They could chew up a bear, clobber it down with a jaw. But I know these American bulldogs well, and they're good dogs. Once upon a time they used to kill bulls for British audiences until the nineteenth century when the government there got soft and made it illegal. He shakes his head, the pool cue in his hand now like a rifle. Then they got to figure out what to do with the dogs. They bred some of them into what's now your cute little condo brat English bulldog, and others they shipped over to the Unites States south where some rednecks taught them a few tricks. Did a pretty good job, I'd say. But they haven't been to Germany as far as I know.

I never told you they came from Germany, Tomas lies. I didn't mean to give you that impression. I only meant that I train them with German techniques.

Oh yeah, I know.

The man uprights his cue stick and chalks it and walks up and leans over the table, aiming, and slams the cue ball into another. They fly about the table. Then he returns and stares at Tomas again.

Tomas runs a nervous finger across his sweaty forehead, beneath his bandanna. Probably he is annoyed with this man for disbelieving him, even though he lied. He wants to do something—hit or yell at him or take the dog off and forget it, but the man had agreed to a price far too high—eight thousand dollars—and Tomas does not want to lose it.

They're techniques I got from the LAPD, Tomas says, trying to hold his stare. You can call my friend on the force right now if you want to. He'd be happy to talk.

The man shakes his head dismissively. There's no need for that. He studies Johan. No. What bothers me is this one's got a small skull. And his cranium above his eyes is too shallow, shows he isn't as smart as his mother.

Tomas starts to speak but the man turns away from him, towards the Mexican lady. What do you think, Lucinda?

She puckers her lips distastefully. I do not care about the size of the skull.

I know you don't.

She comes over and rubs Buster. I like this one.

I could tell you did. Why?

This one, she has a bigger heart than the boy. He is too young and restless. The woman shakes her head as she studies Johan. You will never know how such a young one will turn out.

Tomas looks angry that the maid would interfere with the sale. Actually, he's the quietest one in the litter, he says. Sleeps all night.

She crosses her arms. I don't think so.

My brother must be standing ten feet away from her. He stares at her meanly, keeping his face turned from the man. Hey, do you think you could get us a glass of water or something? he says. It's getting hot in here.

I stiffen.

She does not look pleased. She turns to me. What would you like, little one?

I shrug. A Pepsi?

She nods and does not ask Tomas what he wants and starts towards the kitchen, but the man comes over and touches her shoulder. I'll get it, honey, he says, then looks hard at Tomas. My wife's been busy all morning, he says. I'll get you your water if you're so thirsty.

Tomas's face goes red. His arms hang loosely at his sides.

She's not my maid, you know, the man says.

Tomas attempts not to hesitate. I didn't think she was your maid, mister. I was only thirsty.

The man does not answer my brother but looks towards the window, at the sunbathed mountains and the shadow of a cloud that drifts over its curves and ridges. Sunlight catches a pool table corner.

We just didn't want to get the wrong glasses or anything. Gabe will get us the water.

Hearing my name, I come to attention. All their eyes fall on me.

Sure, I tell them.

No, the man says. I'll get it.

He stops me with a heavy hand and leaves the room. We stand awkwardly with the lady. Tomas occupies himself by rubbing Johan, not looking up. I try to catch his eye but he hides his face from me.

When the man returns he sets the glasses on the bar counter so I have to get them and give one to Tomas. The way the lady watches me I get the feeling she does not think I should have to do this.

The man's arms are crossed, and he stares at Tomas.

Look. I'm paying you eight thousand dollars. I'm overpaying you as it is. Even the mother can't be worth that much.

My brother tries not to look away. Well, she ain't for sale.

Then you'd better leave.

Tomas shifts his weight from one foot to another and his hands are in his pockets. The lady glances at me, then touches the celebrity's arm and says: Wait. I like this dog. The mother.

He looks at her wearily. You really do, honey?

Really.

He scratches the stubble on his chin in a grave and thoughtful manner. You love it?

She nods, turning briefly to me and winking.

He sighs. He turns to Tomas. Okay, son. You heard the woman. She wants this dog. How about I buy both of them from you for the inflated sum of nine thousand dollars each.

Tomas looks like he wants that money real bad. I can't, he finally says, his voice threatening to break.

That's eighteen thousand dollars.

I know it.

You are turning down a lot of money for two dogs.

Tomas looks at his feet, then back up again. I can't.

Well then. How about I pay you eight thousand for the boy dog and twelve thousand for the mother. That's twenty thousand.

Tomas presses his finger into the railing and he watches as his thumb knuckle goes white.

Please, mister. She's a pet. Can't you just buy the boy dog?

My brother has not pleaded with anybody like this in years. Probably not since our father left us, and he had to do a lot of pleading back then. There is almost hurt in his voice and he looks down at Johan. Listen. I promise you I'm not conning you. This one boy dog's my favorite dog next to Buster. His head's small, that's true, but his ears are shaped so you know he's physically balanced and his temples are placed right up to it, not too high or low, which shows he's got a good temperament.

He looks aside and shudders a deep breath. His shirt grows at his chest and his biceps expand outward, to make room, then fall alongside his ribs again. The man studies him for a long time. He finds a checkbook and writes Tomas a check and takes Johan's leash. After rubbing him, he looks at Buster and shakes his head. He dwells on her for a very long time.

I'm sorry. I can understand she's your pet. But if you ever change your mind about this dog, we can deal. I assure you she'd have a good home with her son. You call us. You call *me*.

Sure, Tomas says, pocketing the check.

On our way down the steps he wipes a shoulder against his eyes. It could be the wind—I am not sure—but I am so surprised that without thinking I blurt out, Are you *crying*?

His knuckles hit me hard, so fast I didn't see it coming. My tongue prods at the shreds of my inner cheek, and salty blood floods my mouth.

Jesus, I say, why'd you do that?

Then his fist comes into my gut, sending me forward at the waist, then his elbow comes around the sharp bone of it, sending me sideways onto the driveway, the concrete meeting my temple. The surface feels grainy against my cheek and the torn pieces inside stick to my molars.

Don't you fucking talk disrespect to me.

I wasn't disrespecting you.

Don't you overstand me with your Flip, peasant Spanish.

I was only answering the lady's questions, I start to say, but am interrupted by the bottom of his shoe, the gum and sole and dirt pressing into that part of my face where I feel things the most.

PART
TWO

Dear Ika,

Thank you for your letter of June 27th. We appreciate your prayers, and certainly your boys will be included in our prayers also. Here in Forbes Park life has been taxing but fulfilling. I am preoccupied with duties at the Polo Club and as Eucharist minister at the church, and Millie has been busy herself in redecorating our house in preparation for Malaya's graduation party. It has been not two weeks since Julita's graduation from Ateneo and Millie is very tired. Yet it is so nice to have two daughters earning their degrees at this same time. We are very proud that Malaya will have this master's degree, and from Harvard!

It is with concern that I read of your sons' behavior. In fact, the last time I had seen Tomas I worried greatly even then. You will recall that I suggested to you then that he come to live in the Philippines with me where I could send him to a true Catholic school, one with discipline and supervision, not as those permissive ones which you will find in America. Also, as you know, Millie has a special acquaintance with Professor Inuesto of Ateneo, and Father Reyoso could be of help in gaining admittance for your son(s) as well.

I think you are right to worry about Tomas's influence on his younger brother. It is with great anxiety that I read both of his imitation in dress of his older brother and of their increased fighting. It has been a long time since Gabe has lived in the Philippines. He was very young when he left, and perhaps he does not have a strong sense of his place in this world. Such quiet children can be very impressionable.

I might take this opportunity to suggest that you reconsider and send them here. At Ateneo there would be not only Filipino children but also other mestizos. The problems of kidnapping are greatly exaggerated, mostly confined to Chinese Filipinos, and though the crime is great in Manila generally, here in Forbes Park we are very secluded. I realize that you would not wish to part company with Gabe or Tomas, but it is still possible for you to return to Manila as well. Our country really is not as bad a place as some expatriate Balikbayans might suggest.

I hope to hear from you in the near future on this matter.

You and your sons are in our prayers always.

Love,
Your brother Betino

American Son

somewhere in
Another California
July 1993

Chapter one

I

When my brother wakes up and finds his best breeding dog gone—the one he most loves—and then steps out and finds his 1984 white Oldsmobile missing, it will be a good thing I am out of the San Fernando basin before dawn. Some mornings are like no other. As I drive down the north side of the Los Padres Mountains with a line of semitrailer headlights inching up the opposite lane, the desert spreads out flat before me. The lights of Bakersfield still glitter like an oasis lake reflecting stars I can barely see in the early morning light, and to the left rise the faintly visible Sierra Madres, whose snowy tops catch the still not risen sun.

When I stop at a gas station I use the bathroom but do not wash my hands. They still smell like Buster and I do not want to lose her dog scent smell. It has been a few hours since I stole my brother's dog and sold her, and already I miss her, though there is no way I could turn back now. As I pump gas a family in a white BMW with plates that tell me they bought it in Newport Beach regard my brother's Olds suspiciously. Which tells me they have had encounters with gangs before. They look sporty, the blond boys in back with their colorful windbreakers, crusted with salt and rolled up to their pale knobby elbows. Probably they are on their way up to Mammoth for camping. They look like they might be nice people, but the oldest one mad-dogs me while the gentle-faced smaller one holds on to his brother's arm, then buries his face shyly into his brother's shoulder. They probably think I am Mexican. I hook the pump before the car is filled and pay the attendant and leave.

Instead of taking the 5, I travel up along the eastern part of the state to keep away from the trucks and truck stops and the BMWs with Newport Beach blond boys, or anyone else who might recognize this car. I also don't care for that highway with its dry brown grass that goes on monotonously for miles. It is worse than Palm Springs. You would think with so many people driving up to San Francisco or down to LA someone would plant trees along the road or something. They could make it a nice-looking type of plant you could harvest like broccoli or grapes or carrots. Anyway, this time I am not taking that road.

Here, on the eastern route, the asphalt is not black but a worn sun-beaten silver color and the yellow center line is so faded sometimes you cannot even see it. In some places sand drifts over the highway and you cannot tell exactly where the desert starts and finishes. The towns I pass through are small. Tumbleweed and sheets of sand traverse their streets and bounce off signs that look like they have not been changed since the fifties: Mobil gas signs with the winged horse; men's clothing stores advertising Stetson hats and Wrangler jeans; coffee shops with cardboard squares inside the windows displaying handwritten specials. They are the sort of places my cousin Matt and his Jewish girlfriend like to go to, dragging along their enormous cameras and tripods, to take pictures of people they would not be caught dead hanging out with, but apparently like to look at. Through the fogged windows you can see people inside huddled over their cups, smoking. Noon comes and with it the heat of day. After driving all day I am hungry, but the diners all seem to know each other so I decide to wait for a fast-food place. Night falls, but I do not see any.

After the sun shrivels into the desert, everything below the stars turns black. In the dark, all I see is the desert and asphalt moving beneath my headlights. I do not go by any towns and so begin to worry about finding gas, but there are no cross streets so I do not know exactly where I am on the map. It shows a blank stretch of highway, and I am afraid I might be in it, though probably I am lost. This sort of a place is not supposed to be in California. There are no towns, no malls, no crowds of people, no nothing. No anything. On the black horizon I cannot even tell the difference between the ground and the sky. When I park to pee in the desert, it is so dark I cannot even see my hand before me, nor my shoes. It feels strange and with the howl of wind around me I start imagining coyotes or some other kinds of animals out here, and I wet my hands rushing to zip up and get back into the car.

II

Finally a dome of light swells above the horizon, and I wonder if it is a town or a car approaching from the opposite lane, the first in over an hour.

The first things I see are the lit fifties-era signs of motels and gas stations. One motel has a green and red sign and colored Christmas lights strung along the windows. I fill up with gas and look around for a motel because I am too scared to sleep in the car out in the dark. You never know what the locals might think if they found some stranger sleeping parked on their streets.

A station attendant sells me a sandwich that is wrapped in cellophane and tastes wet and cold after I have peeled off the plastic, and from where I park to eat it you can watch people across the street eating in the diner. Their dinners look better than the sorry thing in my hands. But the tables are full and the men smoke and I feel too shy to go in. There are a couple of older boys with their girlfriends eating, and a group of teenagers hanging out in the parking lot, empty except for their cars. The guys wear these cowboy boots and one of them has a Stetson, his boot heel raised and set on his truck's chrome bumper. I did not know people like this existed in California. They look like they might even listen to country music. I keep in a shadow so they will not see me or Tomas's car, but they do not even look my way. My sandwich bread is soaked with mayonnaise and the thin limp piece of lettuce bunches beneath the cold piece of ham. My teeth crunch on ice where it's been frozen.

I throw the half-eaten lump into a trash can and drive around looking for a motel, but drive up and down the main street and peer down its side streets for ten minutes before realizing that all five of them have no vacancy signs flashing in red. Who would fill these places up is what I want to know. Maybe I should go out and park in the dark roads outside of town. But I am hungry and should eat something first. Otherwise I am liable to wake up in the middle of the night, and hate myself for being a wimp.

Twice I pass down the main street before the diner, peering into its lit booths with its men in plaid shirts and the coatracks with cowboy hats, and the teenagers out front with their pickup truck on huge balloon tires. All the other buildings downtown are dark. A piece of sheet metal clatters against a brick wall, the only noise apart from the distant whistle of wind in the desert.

As I get out of Tomas's car, the dry desert air funnels through the main street buildings. It is bone cold, and I do not have a jacket but jam my hands in my pockets, hurrying towards the lit diner. A couple of boys and their girlfriends exit the main room and step into the little entry room's narrow clutter of hanging coats. Their breath fogs. If they would only hurry up and get out of there, I might not have to run into them. Both boys wear plaid flannel shirts and the girls are blond, one with straight hair and the other with curls. The curly one is the prettiest and scares me the most, and it is her boyfriend whose eyes I evade as I near and enter. In my rush I bump into the pretty girl: even in my confusion I pick up the smell of her perfume amid the rich scent of hamburger grease. It is crowded like a closet in this room and probably I should have waited outside.

I'm sorry, I mumble.

Lifting my glance, I am surprised to see no hostility in her frosty blue eyes, only that she and her boyfriend seem curious, though her attention lasts only a few seconds before she rushes after her friend to tell her something. As they go outside clutching arms and laughing, none of them looks back.

Inside it is warm, like a bathroom after a long shower. The thick smell and sizzle of food is in the air. My glasses fog, and the room becomes a blur: the counter with men hunched over coffee and plates, talking to the waitresses; the booths so close together the families seem shoulder to shoulder; some tarnished plaques on the walls. There are no empty booths and I get the feeling a lone customer should take a stool by the counter. There is no sign telling a person whether they should seat themselves—probably everyone here knows already—so I wait around for a waitress to seat me, but neither of the women approaches. One seems in a hurry, but the younger one with a long rope of wavy brunette hair that sways against the small of her back stops by a booth. Although she holds an order book, she doesn't write anything down but talks to the man with his family. She doesn't seem to be in any hurry, her head tilted towards her shoulder as she laughs at what they say. Several minutes pass. Maybe you are supposed to sit yourself down, but it would seem foolish now to sit after standing all this time, so I do not.

I wipe my glasses, trying to busy my hands. Through the streaked lenses everyone looks mildly alarming, and they seem aware of me.

A woman seems to be glancing my way from the counter where she sits with her husband, but I pretend not to notice. Finally she calls out to me.

Honey, she says. You waiting for someone?

She wears a polyester shirt that bags over her stomach before tucking into her jeans, and a flower pattern is sewn in above her chest pocket.

No, I say.

She regards me curiously.

Well what you waitin' for?

I shrug. A seat.

Well, hon, the booths are all taken. You better find yourself a place at the counter.

Okay.

I sit down and turn my coffee cup right side up and bury

my head in the plastic menu, listening to the murmur around me and trying to take everything in without looking up.

I smell warm coffee and look up and the waitress with long brunette hair is filling my cup. She goes off before I can order, carelessly splashing liquid that runs caramel-colored down the white porcelain and puddles on the countertop.

I feel the woman with the flower pattern looking at me and she calls out from her table.

Honey, she says. Where you coming from?

Los Angeles.

Is that so?

I nod.

You visiting relatives here?

No.

So you got yourself a motel, honey, I hope. We got the car races up in Oregon tomorrow and all the motels are full.

That's okay.

So you got a place to stay?

I shrug.

She looks at me and her eyes widen and she makes a frown and taps out her cigarette. Oh, honey. I hope you aren't planning on driving on tonight. It's a long way to Medford. Over a hundred miles.

No I'm not, I lie.

So you got yourself a hotel. Good. Your parents know you're up here? They give you money to pay for it?

Sure.

And you found yourself a hotel.

It's up the road.

All right then.

The waitress comes and I order some eggs and pancakes and she brings them and they steam in my face and I can taste the cheese in the eggs and put Tabasco sauce on my plate and dip them in and I even lick the grease clean off my fork. Then I drink some water and tip ice onto my tongue to wash out the good greasy taste and wait for my bill. The woman who talked to me earlier is trying to call to me again. It is no use ignoring her.

So where you driving to, honey?

Up north, I say.

This woman makes it sound like we are close to Oregon, which is about two or three hundred miles north of where I intended to drive, so it is probably better not to tell her that I am trying to get to San Francisco.

You going to Medford, honey? she says.

No.

Yeah, I didn't think a young guy like you would want anything to do with Medford. It's all old Californians up there. Retired.

To this I nod as if I knew where the place was.

Her husband has gotten up and paid the bill, but she does not follow him and seems in no hurry. The man takes a seat at the far end of the counter and asks the waitress for a glass of water, then does not drink from it as he stares at the wall.

The woman says: So you are going up to Portland, I suppose.

I do not contradict her.

Got a girlfriend there, I guess. Or maybe college. You look like you're a college type.

This woman must be blind. I am years too young. Maybe it's because around here there are no colleges and everyone from out of town must look like a college person to her.

You don't seem like most of the rotten types we get from down there, she says.

Thank you.

It's mostly trashy plastic types we get. All kinds of garbage.

It's a crummy place.

She nods, approvingly. She signals to the waitress and asks her to bring me a chocolate sundae which she says I should try, and the waitress brings it and they watch me eat. It tastes like cool lumps of syrup on my tongue and I scrape the metal dish clean and then they do not let me pay for it. After it is gone I can see the dish marks on the countertop where condensation lay. The waitress runs a rag across it and it is gone.

So what motel you staying in, honey? the first woman says.

Oh, I'm just going up the road.

But what's the name of the hotel? I hope it isn't the Deer Trader.

Nope.

Where then?

I'm driving on tonight, I finally mumble.

What was that?

I'm driving on tonight.

Now that's funny. I could of sworn you just said you had yourself a hotel room.

My fingertips cradle my wet glass of ice water. I just drove by one and thought I might take a room, I say. But then you told me they were all taken. So I guess I'll drive on.

Well, drive safe anyway. I wish I could offer you a couch to sleep on, a sweet-looking boy like you, but my brother-in-law is visiting.

That's okay.

She seems to want to say something but hesitates for a long time, looking at me. She finally says: I got a mattress on the porch you can sleep on. It's a bit weathered—you know, yellowed from the rain—but it's late and you might be tired.

Thanks. But I'm in a hurry to meet someone.

In Portland?

Yeah.

She nods half to herself and we are silent but still she does not go to her husband. Time passes. The door opens and lets in a cool curtain of air. The diners hug themselves and huddle against one another. There is the smell of biscuits I love so, like what Mom learned to fix my dad—the way Grandma Sullivan made them—and in this hot room the windows steam, and people talk across the tables. Finally the waitress comes and sets my bill on the counter, minus the sundae, and I wait awhile in the warm room with the smell and talk and clatter of dishes scraped clean but I get the feeling people are waiting on me to leave. So I pay at the register and stand in the warm doorway for a moment before entering the cool night and driving out of town. My fingers stick to the cold plastic steering wheel. It hurts to peel them off.

Behind me the town's light sucks down into the darkness and then there is only the black desert around me when the car begins making jerking noises and, finally, twenty minutes later, breaks down.

III

When I wake up my back hurts from my seat's awkward position and I sit up straight. To my surprise I am not surrounded by desert. Outside, long grass stands uncut at the roadside, in yellow clumps that form a nest for the newly risen sun, and barbed wire strung between old wooden posts separates a field from the road. The fields are hilly, some low sort of vegetation, with the early light glistening in ponds and irrigation streams like clear thread among quilted patches. A jackrabbit runs across the narrow road, darting into a patch of bush. Three deer leap over the barbed wire onto the road and jump to the opposite field and hurry up the green hills, becoming silhouettes against the blue sky. It happens so fast, when they are gone, I doubt I have even seen them.

I get out and stretch. The air is cold in my throat— mountain air—and my breath fogs, billows, and vanishes before my face. The Oldsmobile starts on the first try, which surprises me. Remembering what that woman said about being near Oregon, I decide to backtrack to Navarro. As I take the road the gas seems to sputter, so I try to coast most of the way in neutral. By the time I come into town the car is barely moving and I just make it into one of the only two service stations I have seen in town. They face each other and one looks more open than the other. An aluminum garage door with its slotted glass windows has been rolled up halfway and some guy sits inside behind a desk, and he has long beige hair.

I step into the cool dark room of cars raised towards the ceiling, into the smell of dust and oil. A silent television up on the wall lights the dust in flickering colors and shines on his face. My worn sneakers nearly slip on the smooth cement.

The man does not stand.

I ask him if he will take a look at my car. He peers at me curiously, then walks outside into the sunlight and stands as I pop the hood. He gazes inside it, hands behind his back, not touching anything, as if he were only observing.

I describe the way the gas felt when I touched the pedal, the sputtering motions. He does not volunteer anything, and finally I ask him if he thinks he knows what is wrong with it.

You say you bought gas last night? he says.

Yeah.

Could be bad gas if it's true the car started sputtering after you bought it like you said.

So you think it could be the gas?

I doubt it. We don't sell bad gas. Nobody's complained, and believe me, people would've complained if we'd sold them bad gas.

He frowns at the thought of complaining people, and his red tongue comes out and licks at his chapped lip.

I didn't buy it from here, I say. I bought it down the road.

He shakes his head. Same truck that fills that station fills ours. The only thing might be if their tank was almost empty. When it got filled it might have kicked up sediment. That could've clogged your feeder.

So you think that's it?

No.

I wait for the man to say something more, but he only shades his face and tucks his long bangs beneath his cap, against his blistered ear. He never stops regarding me.

Well, so what do you think it is? I say.

No idea.

The man walks around Tomas's Oldsmobile, peering curiously at the oversize tires, the lowered shocks, the white paint that covers even the chrome on the bumpers. At home it seems like a normal car to have, but here I feel like throwing a damned blanket over it. He touches nothing, like if he did he might have to try and fix it.

So do you know anyone who can fix it? I say.

He glares up from the passenger window, into which he has been looking.

Sure.

And who is it?

The man smiles to himself, shaking his head as if I had reminded him of something amusing.

You'll have to ask the owner, he says. He does all the work.

Okay.

He ain't here, though.

The man does not offer to tell me where the owner is. He just looks at me.

Okay, when will he be in? I say.

Oh, he don't work on weekends. It's Saturday.

You're kidding.

Nope.

What about the place across the street? You know if they'll open up today?

They won't.

You sure about that?

The same guy who fixes everything here owns that place too, he says.

You mean it's the same guy?

He's my boss.

The station across the street is a Chevron, unlike this one, and looks newer, but I do not have any reason to doubt this man. I do not think he would lie mostly to get my business. The way he watches me curiously, he does not exactly seem impatient to get back to his desk.

So you mean no place is open here on weekends, not even Saturday?

That's right, he says.

Look, I say. You think if I pay him he'll come out?

Ha! Not on your life.

I tap my foot restlessly. But you might know where he is, where I might call him.

He's out hunting, but if I gave you his number he'd kill me, the man says, with his amused-looking smile. He asks where I'm from and I tell him Los Angeles. That seems to amuse him more and he starts asking questions and I answer as few as possible and then ask him what he thinks I should do. He tells me that because it is the Fourth of July weekend I will have to wait until Tuesday and even then they might have to order a part.

You telling me I can't do anything?

You can go down the street and yell at those guys who gave you gas.

Do they know how to fix a car?

No.

I ask him if I can leave the car in his lot and he says yes and I walk five blocks to the only pay phone in town. The air is dry and parched and dusty and by the time I get there filmy dust covers my tongue. There are only three men who tow in the region and one of them tells me he could put a hundred miles on my brother's AAA card and charge me for the rest. He recommends towing across the state border to Medford, Oregon. But he cannot make it before one o'clock.

I do not feel like yelling at the guy at the station that sold me gas, and I do not want the attendant to ask me why I have not yelled at them, so I do not return to my car but sit on the parking lot's low cinder-block wall, chin on my palms. Across the blacktop, with its yellow clumps of brittle weeds pushing through asphalt cracks, is the diner. In the daylight I now see it is a shiny chrome color, built in the shape of a large trailer, and inside slanted sunlight outlines shadows over mostly empty booths. A back door is open, the sound of sizzling grease comes to my ears, and there is the sharp smell of burning hamburger patties, which makes me approach. But a woman sitting at the counter comes into view, and although I cannot see her face, it is possible that she is the woman I talked to last night. I do not want her to know I am not in Portland, Oregon, with some girlfriend. So I walk into the residential streets and try to keep in the shade of occasional trees—running from one patch of them to another—across hot bright sidewalks, just killing time. Through the warped screened porches, sometimes I can see that the owners have left their doors open. Something you would not see in my neighborhood.

A thick, sticky pollen seems to fall from the branches, whose leaves hang limp like algae. As I spoon frozen yogurt I bought at a convenience store, I carve white moons from the yellow pollen-covered surface. It leaves a dusty taste on my tongue. Sometimes kids run by me, always white and unattended by adults. Two girls with a bicycle trying to teach a boy how to ride it without training wheels. Two boys who stop me and ask for advice on baseball cards even though I am a stranger. One block in particular seems like a good place to live, and I find myself coming back to it. Behind the houses, farmland stretches out green and rolling. Wind catches and clatters a loose porch screen, tapping pleasantly. To live here it must be cheap. Mom could sleep by the front windows here, without worrying about any Johnny Guerro types; she could even sleep out on the porch on warm summer evenings. The stars would be visible and

clear above the leafy treetops and the streets quiet and careless. There could not be too many jobs here, but anything
beats her current job and surely houses could be bought for
cheap. During the rest of the afternoon I wonder what kind
of lives the people in these places must have, where the
young people go at night.

Chapter two

I

For an hour, I wait around the side of the cinder-block service station so the attendant will not see me and try to talk. About twelve-thirty, the tow truck pulls in. It is a shimmering black Ford, its platform so huge an SUV could ride on it. It has wide chrome bumpers. It has a grille along which sparks of sun slide as it humps the curb and maneuvers to back before my car. It is as polished as a fire truck, and the newness of the vehicle so startles me that I hesitate, not certain it is for me. By the time I run up, the driver has been honking at the attendant with the long greasy hair.

The man struts up to the truck, a soiled cloth hanging out of his back pocket and swinging like a horsetail, shading his eyes as he peers up.

They start a conversation so I slow to a walk, then stop several feet away. Maybe I should interrupt and tell the man it is my car, but I do not want to be rude. The platform-truck driver gets out, still talking, and steps down from the chrome footrail and lands on the asphalt. Though he makes the landing easily enough, his flannel shirt—torn to be short-sleeved—does nothing to hide his beer belly, and the red bandanna wrapped around his forehead matches the pockmarks on his cheeks. His crusty jeans are so threadbare they shine as they rub upon his thighs. His arms appear hard and I can make out the shape of his muscles as they move beneath his freckled skin, and the biker tattoos along his arms. The men seem to know each other and talk about common acquaintances.

Soon it becomes obvious the tow truck guy is waiting around for whoever owns Tomas's car. For some reason the attendant does not tell him it's me. They exchange words about the vintage-car races up in Oregon, and the fleet of old colorful cars that drove in yesterday afternoon and took over the town, filling up the motels and bars. It seems awkward for me to say anything at this point, and I feel weird just watching this conversation. Several times the truck driver glances my way, probably wondering why I am listening. Finally, possibly because of me, he announces that he is going to give up on the owner and leave, and begins to turn towards his truck.

He has turned before I can signal to him, and the gas attendant looks curiously at me but does not say a word. I call to the tow truck driver.

He stops with a boot on the footrail and asks me who I am. I tell him I own the car.

Why the hell didn't you say something? he says with a smile. I nearly left.

Sorry.

You're the one who would've been without a tow. Don't be sorry to me.

He fastens a chain end under the Oldsmobile's bumper and a motor drags it up onto the platform. It stands up there like an advertisement for Los Angeles gangsterdom, bright white against the blue sky. The man does not give it a second look, though.

From inside the cab you can see the roofs of the cars we pass, and as we turn onto the main street you can see right into the laps of drivers and all the items on their seats, and into the dirty beds of rust-crusted pickup trucks. Nobody can hide. The cab smells strongly of pine, which comes from a little plastic tree that dangles from the rearview mirror. After hesitating for a long time I roll down the window and let in warm fresh air that blows against my forehead, dries my eyes, and makes me squint. The tow truck man drives and looks forward, whistling occasionally. A few times he glances my way. Maybe I should not have opened the window. Wind rattles a piece of paper stuck like a bee above the dashboard and I think about closing it but do not.

I feel the man thinking about me. Finally he turns my way.

Sorry about that, he says. You looked too young to be driving a big old Olds like that one. I expected some sort of a grandpa.

My grandpa gave it to me, I lie to him.

He nods to himself.

In Culver City or Venice no grandpa with any brains would leave his ten-year-old gas-guzzling Olds parked on the street. Apart from a Land Cruiser, it's what everyone wants to steal. It is obvious that though he deals with cars, this man does not know anything about LA gangs and their car habits. I let my shoulders slack a little.

That's a nice grandpa, he says.

Yeah, I know.

We drive without a word along the main street, then begin the upward slant towards the foothills, passing beneath a traffic light that arches over the street like a gateway. Again I sense the man glancing my way, and automatically I shrug as if the feeling I get from it were a bird on my shoulder.

Finally he says: Why didn't you say anything back there? It must've been obvious I was looking for the owner of your car.

I don't know.

He regards me curiously, then smiles and laughs. All right then. That makes two of us. You thirsty? Why don't you reach back behind your seat and pull out the cooler. Have yourself what you want.

Thanks.

The foam lid comes off the chest and feels cold in my fingers, and the icy air rises to my face. Wet ice slides down my chosen can of root beer, bunching above my fingers, and I can barely restrain myself from opening it while getting his can of Budweiser, I am so hungry. First I pop his open and hand it to him, then finally pop my own can and put the cold metal to my lips before it stops hissing. The sugar seems to enter my bloodstream right away. My lips peel free from the cold metal.

Boy you're thirsty, he says.

I set the can between my thighs and turn to him and nod.

Don't stop now, he says. Go at it, buddy.

I drink.

We stop at the gas station I pulled into last night. Maybe I should warn him about bad gas. When you know something that could hurt someone or their truck you should say something about it, but for some reason I do not. And I do not want the tow truck guy to know I should be complaining to the gas guy either, so I duck lower in my seat so the attendant cannot see me. The tow truck guy offers to go inside and buy me something to eat. I tell him no thanks, but later see him paying for a candy bar.

When he passes my window on his way to the pump, he hands the candy bar up casually, as though we are old buddies and there is no need to thank him. From the way he looks you would think he was some sort of a local biker or redneck, but something about the way he did this seems familiar, and as he moves about his truck he seems different from the other people you see in this town. Just as I am wondering whether he is from Los Angeles and maybe he will recognize something about Tomas's car, I notice a USC emblem dangling from his key chain.

The pump clicks off and the metal nozzle scrapes the truck as he takes it out of the tank, then he opens his door.

Getting into the cab and reaching for the ignition, he says, You're a quiet type, aren't you?

I nod.

He thinks this over.

That's a good trait to have, he says.

We turn back onto the main street and pass an old sooty brick building whose black tar roof glitters in the sunlight. In the distance the mountains are white-capped. Patches of snow peer out brilliantly from within the bowls and crags of granite faces, and seem to flicker as we move.

That's a pretty strange trait for someone who comes from Los Angeles.

I guess so.

You don't seem like the LA type, he says, stretching his arm to rest it upon his window like a cowboy in a western. I stretch out my own arm and rest it the same way, but the plastic is too high and feels hard against the knob of my elbow. As he smokes a cigarette the smoke glows in the sunlight and drifts out the crack above the window in a thin sheet.

So you wondering how I know you're from LA? he says.

I wasn't really, but I tell him sure.

I saw the road maps in your backseat, he says. I hope you don't mind I peered in.

No.

Sure, buddy. I could tell you're an easy sort of guy. I knew you wouldn't.

He puts a hand on my shoulder and even through my shirt his heavy palm feels moist and wet. He squeezes. As we drive towards the edge of town into the early slant of the foothills my body seems more relaxed than it has in a long time. As he waves at a passing driver, an old woman with a mound of white hair, I almost wave too.

Then he speaks without taking his eyes off the faded asphalt, That's too bad for you.

What?

You know, that you come from Los Angeles.

I nod.

Fucking shithole if you ask me.

We pass a German shepherd rummaging through an overturned trash can. I tightly grip the plastic door handle.

Sure it is, I say.

Crime. Traffic. You don't get that kind of idiocy up here.

No?

Not a bit.

He waits for something more.

Sounds great, I tell him.

So you like it down there?

I guess not.

He nods approvingly. You know I'm from San Bernardino originally, he says. Lived there, Riverside, San Pedro. You must know those places.

Yeah, I lie.

Too bad for you.

He slaps his thigh and leans forward laughing.

Yeah, shitholes both, he adds. San Pedro especially.

He looks at me like he wants me to say something about San Pedro, some special detail, and I try to think of names of avenues but my pulse beats beneath my wrist and I can't think of anything. I slide up in my seat.

Yeah, I say. It's a crappy place.

This seems to make him feel better, like I have helped him picture San Pedro in his mind. He talks about San Bernardino and Riverside and I tell him they suck too. He gets worked up. He fingers his damp bandanna off his fore-head, then wipes the sweat off with the back of his hand and it comes away with drops of moisture glistening on the fine little hairs.

Despite his flannel shirt with a Harley patch and his bandanna, now that I know where he is from something about him seems obviously Los Angeles, something in the way he moves and the way he speaks. He says he used to be a mechanical engineer in an auto plant. He doesn't look like my idea of an engineer. I ask him about this and he tells me he has done a bunch of things and even used to be a work-ing actor.

He asks me about San Bernardino. I stiffen, knowing nothing, but then think to tell him Venice is worse. He nods and seems satisfied.

Venice is a shithole, he says.

I nod.

Bunch of fucking Mexicans.

I keep quiet. In the rearview mirror I can see Tomas's white Oldsmobile, the white painted bumpers and the black tires shining in the mountain sunlight. This guy obviously doesn't know about Oldsmobiles. Hopefully nobody will know about them in any gas stations we might pass.

Am I wrong? he says.

It's true.

He shakes his head, gripping the steering wheel, getting excited. Sunlight catches the little hairs on his arm and they look blond and almost reddish and I can see where the muscles move beneath. But it isn't near as bad as San Pedro, he says. Cambodians, Vietnamese, Laotians.

I say nothing.

Am I right? he says.

Sure.

All those mute Asians won't even learn to speak English.

My pulse beats in my neck and my temples and my fingertips. My eyes avoid the rearview mirror as a hot itchiness grows in my underarms and I want to take off my sweater. He must be blind. Maybe it's because of my clothes and the way I now cut my hair. Outside the yellow sun hangs over the mountain range. A hazy smudge of burnt color. We pass low spindly pine trees and a wide mesa plain covered by clusters of shaggy cactus in prickly silhouette. A honking caravan of vintage cars approaches from the opposite lane— two black and three yellow—and they flash by and disappear behind us.

He taps the steering wheel with his fingertips, clicking the plastic. He begins to whistle.

After a while he looks at me: You want another root beer, Gabe? You drank the last one up pretty good.

I shake my head.

Maybe later.

I nod.

He regards me.

You know, I hope it didn't bother you what I said about them Asians being quiet. I think it's good you're a quiet guy. More people should learn to listen, is what I say.

Sure.

I didn't mean to make any judgments about quiet people, per se.

I know.

It's just when these people come to this country and won't learn English, how can a person like that listen? No, it's a different thing.

Maybe I'll have that root beer, I say.

Sure, buddy, he says, leaning back. He lifts the ice chest lid for me this time. The can snaps open and hisses. He hands it to me. The can is slippery with ice and nearly slides out from my hand and I steady it and thank him.

It's just people like that made me want to move up here, he says.

I know what you mean.

You do?

Yeah.

He thinks about this and nods. We pass through a thinning in the trees and dappled light illuminates his face followed by a sharp light which then slowly fades. I notice where shadows fall beneath his eyes from worry. We round a curve and his face catches the sun again and I notice that his glowing stubble has red ends and they cover wrinkles at the edges of his mouth.

So you like it up here? I say.

Sure.

It sounds nice that you don't have any crime. Where we live it's a big problem for my mom.

Is that right?

Yeah.

He shakes his head, true concern on his face.

She has to sleep in the back of our house because of drive-by shootings, I say.

You can't be serious.

Oh yeah, I nod. We get all kinds. The Mexicans come up and it's like they're still roaming all the barrios killing each other down in Mexico. They have their neighborhoods they mark up with graffiti. Like pissing dogs. The new ones have macho mustaches and slick their hair back like they're some kind of Spanish Casanovas, but they're like these short Indian-looking guys. The Cambodians are the worst. It's like their war isn't over yet.

You know, he says, getting excited, his eyes widening, I really know what you mean.

Suddenly he looks upon me with fatherly concern. An overwhelming warmth spreads within me like an intake of hot sour breath. Blushing, I turn away.

He leans forward and fingers open his top shirt button, barely able to restrain himself. A gold chain connects to a pendant which rests against a nest of chest hair. He pulls it out.

Here, take a look at this, he says, handing it to me.

The warm sweaty metal feels heavy in my fingers. It takes a moment of fumbling for the latch to snap open. There's a picture of a pretty blond girl inside.

He seems to be nervously studying me as if to see what I think of her.

Who's this? I finally say.

She was my daughter.

The photo is a cutout from a color snapshot and you can see where the edges were trimmed with scissors to make it oval. She looks about twenty and is smiling and you can see her baby fat beneath her pale skin and she wears some sort of a fitted suit and looks nothing like this man. I want to ask him what he means by "was," but I do not.

He unbuttons his shirt further, then peels back the damp fabric to reveal more of his chest. Matted chest hair clings to the shirt wool, then pops back. It seems weird that he would do this, and I look down.

Look here, he says.

There is a quarter-sized red scar on his chest, and suddenly he takes my hand in his sweaty palm and leads my finger to it. I have to force myself not to jerk away, this is so surprising. His black chest hair feels thick against my fingertip, the skin warm. A pulse beats, though I do not know whether it is his or mine.

It's a bullet hole, he finally says.

I do not know what you are supposed to say to something like this. Some people seem to have words for everything, but not me. In my throat a lump swells and ebbs. I cannot even get myself to ask how it happened.

I'm telling you, buddy, he says, buttoning back up. You should think about moving your mom to this place. She sounds like a real nice lady.

II

We come out of a hilly forest onto a high plateau meadow of grass which glows light green in the sunlight, and my words will no longer come. We ride quietly. Having no words makes me nervous and I glance at him and then quickly back to forward and I do this again several times and then finally I ask him how come things are so safe around here.

It seems to me with so few people around you could not get away with any mischief without people noticing and anyway people wouldn't be so cramped and uptight and crazy, but this question feels like something which would please him. He tells me the locals keep it clean. That there is not a mall or a McDonald's for a hundred miles. Only decent people live around here.

But how do you keep undesirables out? I say, adding that my mother's safety makes this of particular interest to me.

He shifts excitedly. You know how journalists keep coming up here to study reports of alien abductions?

Yeah.

Well there's plenty of abductions, but it isn't aliens that do it.

I keep still. Menace fills the cab like steam in a shower and we pass an old meadow of brittle brown grass and an abandoned shack sits at the edge of it, the windows slotted, by a tight cluster of ragged trees. Their branches look like the teeth of an old rusted saw. Our tires crackle over a patch of windblown gravel, then continue their smooth rubber hum.

These locals are crazy, he says. They take troubles into their own hands. When undesirables come up, they tell them to get lost, and if they don't, that's their own peril.

We come into large fields of low alfalfa traversed by long shining pipes standing on tripods, spraying water each thirty yards. Rainbow colors glow faintly in the mist. Probably there are a million places you could buy a plot of land and build a small house and live for really cheap. So many people live in dumpy little houses in LA and complain about smog and crime and even about all the complaining people. Why they stay there I do not know. This could be a farm like where Mom grew up. Only no peasants live on the land. No people for hundreds of yards, no groups of them for many miles to bother you.

So they keep it safe here, I tell him.

Sure.

That's good.

The man notices me nod approvingly as I stare out the window.

I've lived here eight years since it happened, he says, pausing. It is clear he means something about the bullet and his dead daughter. We are quiet and I want to say something to make him feel better. We pass a sixteen-wheeler whose wind shakes and rattles our cab. I tell him some rotten stories about LA so he can think about how much better things are for him now, though I am careful not to ask him about his daughter. Watching Tomas has given me plenty to talk about, though I do not tell him he is my brother but make it seem like the gangsters I describe are just people I have seen in school.

He shakes his head, bewildered. That's a hell of a childhood to live through, he says.

I let him sympathize for me, lowering my head towards my lap. In this way I do not have to put another word in for twenty miles.

III

He tries to tell me about hunting trips he used to take with his brother, which is how he found out about this region originally, though he finally falls silent. He seems preoccupied and, sensing him glance my way a couple of times, I wonder if he is worried about the ordeals I have to go through being a school kid in Venice. To tell the truth, I only lasted in Venice High less than a week. I feel bad I told him those stories. At one point, out of the blue, he tells me the girl in the locket picture was his only kid. I do not know what to say to this—it seems weird he would keep telling me this sort of thing. His worrying fills the car, which reminds me of driving with Mom. She will worry about me like crazy.

Look, buddy, he says. We're coming to the place I told you about. Let me buy you lunch.

You don't have to do that.

Oh it's no problem.

This is the first time I have ever heard of a tow truck driver buying his customer lunch, but for some reason he keeps insisting. He will not take no for an answer and seems to get sore so I keep quiet.

He parks in a dirt lot and we head towards an old diner.

Though the wall-like windows are tinted, walking towards the restaurant I can see faintly within a few people sitting in booths.

Suddenly I notice my reflection in the mirrored glass and it appears so obviously Asian I almost stop in my tracks. My eyes look narrow, and my hair straight and coarse and black. He must be blind. I have slender Asian hips, and my cheekbones are too high. The way the sunlight hits my face you cannot even make out my eyes. My eyes jerk away. Everyone will be able to tell. I might even look Mexican, but not white. My heart thumps in my throat—if someone recognizes me after what I said to him about Asians—I don't know. I avoid the tow truck guy's face—

annoyed that he didn't notice and keep me out of this place with its people. The idea of firing him or insisting on waiting in the cab even occurs to me—my *right*—but that seems ridiculous. Suddenly I stop before the door.

He turns and looks at me. What's the matter, buddy? Aren't you coming in?

I look towards the truck which sits unlocked in the sunlight.

Sure, I tell him.

Inside, the tinted glass makes the room darker. My eyes relax after the outdoor straining but immediately dart around to see if anyone is studying me. A number of people sit in booths of crusted brown vinyl, but they do not look our way and we sit at the counter.

As he sits his jeans move loosely over his wide thighs, and his faint reflection appears on the polished countertop. He sets down his elbows and leans forward.

Susan, he calls out.

A waitress enters the room from the kitchen door and struts our way, fingering her large earrings.

Hey-llo, Stone, she says, then looks down at me. Who's your friend?

His name is Gabe.

As she gently scrutinizes my face, my eyes find the countertop. She seems to sense something strange but breaks into a smile. She is a person who looks young for her age—smooth skin, but with something older in her eyes—and her forearm is so delicate you can see light blue veins beneath her arms.

Nice to meet you, Gabe.

She asks me what I want to eat and I tell her a hamburger and the man makes his order and tells her to add fries and a chocolate sundae to mine and she goes off into the kitchen. While she is out of the room I relax a little, noticing that near the ceiling the walls are bare drywall and the carpeting is not wall-to-wall, but one beige piece spread upon bare concrete. When she comes back he has told me the prices of housing in the area, in case my good mother decides she would like to consider relocating. As the waitress nears us, I try to get him off the topic (in case she might put location and face together and think I look like an Asian or Mexican) by bringing up a hunting discussion we covered earlier.

He ignores me by turning to the lady and telling her I'm from Los Angeles but I'm different and what a smart kid I am to listen to.

She looks at me, So you're from Los Angeles?

I nod.

Yeah, we get a lot of travelers coming through, she says. I don't think too much of most of them.

Oh, he's okay, the man says.

She pretends to scrutinize me: You'd better not be too nice to the boy, Stone. He might have a rich mother who'll come up and jack up our housing prices.

She winks at me and thucks down a water glass. Ice clicks against the sides.

The man tells her my mother has to sleep in the living room due to unprovoked drive-by Asian gang shootings, but I do not remind him it is really that the gangs are Mexican—which I had told him—or that they are mad at me and my brother—which I had not.

The waitress shakes her head sympathetically and clicks her tongue. She seems about to say something but the door opens, letting in a breeze and a sharp flood of daylight, making her face and the room glow like breath-blown embers. She frowns as she sees a teenage girl coming in, and without a word she walks off and puts her head into the kitchen door, as if she were preoccupied.

The girl sits right next to us, shifting about as she gets comfortable on her stool and setting a handbag on the counter, her leather strap drooping off the edge. She opens a plastic menu.

The waitress comes back, ignoring the girl.

It sounds like you know how to take care of your good mother, she says to me. She is speaking very loudly.

She doesn't pay attention when I nod, but steps in front of the girl. Suddenly she takes the menu from the girl's hands.

The girl looks up. Why'd you do that?

You know what's on the menu, Becky. Just tell me what you want.

The girl looks at her in disbelief. *They* know what's on it, she says, gesturing toward some men in a corner booth, But you don't take menus away from *them*.

You gonna order, Becky, or what?

Oh, did you forget? You already know what I want. I always get the same thing.

The waitress sighs. With a hand on her hip, she just looks at the girl. The girl seems to feel her stare.

What? she says.

So you gonna pay for it?

The girl rolls her eyes. It's your money. If you want to throw it away, fine.

The woman glances around, as if embarrassed the girl would talk so disrespectfully in front of others. It's just that you seem to want to be treated exactly like any paying customer, you're so grown up.

Fuck you.

The waitress reaches over and slaps the girl's water glass on its side, sending ice sliding across the counter. She throws a rag on the puddle and walks into the kitchen.

The girl swears to herself, then under her breath adds the word *bitch*.

We all sit quietly. So far the girl hasn't paid me much attention. With the waitress gone, I tense, just waiting for her to look over at me. It is always young people more than grown-ups who notice there is something about me. The girl does not touch the rag, and water runs along the table in a spreading puddle. The tow truck guy reaches for the rag and mops the mess up, although it gets soaked before he can sop up all the water. Some drips onto my lap and I have no napkin and am too embarrassed to ask for one, so I stop the cold liquid and sliding cubes with a finger, then roll my wrist sideways to sop it discreetly with a sleeve. Perhaps this will not draw the girl's attention. But as I sense her glance my way, my hand stops. The tow truck guy seems embarrassed and pretends not to notice. It is obvious, though, that we are both aware of this girl sitting there.

Finally the waitress comes back. She sets down our plates with a distracted plastic smile and then snaps up her rag. Mist sprays across my face. She disappears again.

Bitch, the girl says.

The man's left cheek twitches violently, followed by a slight shudder of his shoulders. He doesn't say anything though.

We eat quietly, then the waitress returns. She seems slightly aloof and embarrassed now, even while she tries to make small talk with us. She wipes up the counter as she tries to trade words with the tow truck guy, pointedly ignoring the girl. If only she would not mention where I am from in front of the daughter. But finally she does, saying something about teenagers being no better here than in LA.

The girl squints evilly her way. Then, her eyes slide toward me and begin taking note of me for the first time. They hesitate on my face as I eat, carefully. She knows something. On her wrist she has a strange, slug-sized, delicate tattoo and her fingernails have the chipped faded remnants of black fingernail polish. It is all I can do to keep spooning food into my mouth.

You're from LA? she says.

Sort of.

What do you mean sort of?

Santa Monica.

Is that your Olds on the back of the tow truck?

Heads turn towards the window to the truck where the Olds sits high upon its back, bright as a seashell's interior.

Why'd you paint the chrome white like that? she says after not getting a response.

No reason.

Well, there must be some reason.

Because it looks good.

No it doesn't.

She expects an answer. The tow truck man pretends to study his sandwich.

Let the boy eat, her mother interrupts.

The girl says something unkind and gets up and leaves the room, thank God. The waitress looks after her and picks up her glass and silver and drops them clattering into a dish bucket and mumbles something about the ignorance of young people but seems visibly relaxed now. The man is deadly still. The sandwich remains uneaten on his plate. The waitress mumbles something about the girl being a little bitch and the man excuses himself and goes into the bathroom. She looks after him, her rag hanging limply in her hand. When he comes back she asks if I am old enough for coffee, and the man answers yes for me, and she flips over the cups and fills them both. It smells good and warm and you can take the aroma in deeply.

That's it kid, he says. Drink up.

He takes me around the booths and introduces me to the people he knows as I follow him around. Something about this feels weird, like maybe it is the way a man would show off his son, and as people look at me curiously I wonder if they know about the dead daughter. He seems to expect me to stand beside him like a statue on display. But as we move around the tables I find myself not minding that he would introduce me like this. Maybe I even feel a little proud, keeping close beside him as men reach out and shake my hand, or just nod at me. To those people he does not know, the waitress introduces us with a few sharp words, giving each man a sarcastic title, making them chuckle. In the corner booth he makes references to the gangs my mother has to endure. When he refers to Mexicans, an old man whose hand shakes from age as it holds a cigarette looks away from him as if from embarrassment. The old guy taps his cigarette and stares out the window.

IV

Now I suppose it is possible the old guy thought I was Mexican. Or maybe he did not like Stone saying these sorts of things, or he could even have hated Stone. I wouldn't know, but I got the feeling we should leave, though Stone stuck around talking to the old guys, who obviously did not want him there. I have noticed that lots of times people have no clue where they are welcome or not, though that has not been my problem—at least, I know when to leave, although maybe not necessarily when to stay.

After all, I would have gotten out of there the second the old guy turned towards the window, but later when we got onto the topic of hunting outside Navarro, the man turned back to him and you could see the interest in his eye. This seemed to satisfy Stone—seemed to give him what he wanted—and soon after, we left. Me, I don't know that all that nervousness was worth it for a couple of sentences exchanged about hunting.

In some way, though, I got the feeling he wanted those old guys to like him, in front of me.

He takes me into the kitchen to tour the facilities. Why he would do this, I do not know. The cook and dishwasher are Mexican and, away from the old men, the moodiness of a moment ago seems to have left him. The long steel counter is cluttered with glinting dishes, and a back door opens to daylight which seems to give the doorframe a rectangular halo. The brightness makes everything inside the kitchen appear slightly blurry.

It seems strange that he would want to show me the kitchen, but he does and seems proud of it, and finally explains that he owns a small part of the restaurant, a very small part. As he shows me around, the two Mexicans look upon him with their arms crossed, and once they trade amused glances behind his back. They appear only a few years older than me. Though I try to avoid their eyes, once the cook seems to wink at me, though afterwards I am not sure if this really happened. They should not take such liberties. Finished with the tour, Stone tries to think if there is anything left to show me. Not thinking of anything, he still seems reluctant to leave. They are watching us. A tap drips water and a bird chirps shrilly outside. The branches of a leafless tree appear dark and thin against the clean sky. This man, he must be blind.

My eyes ease towards the sunny back doorway where I would like to go, but he just leans against the counter lost in his mind. The Mexican workers trade more looks.

Maybe we should go now, I say.

He seems to pull himself out of his thoughts, looking up at me.

Sure, buddy, he mumbles distractedly.

I start towards the door to the main room, but he nods at the back door. Why don't you go out the back and I'll just use the bathroom. I'll splash some water on my face and meet you outside.

I hesitate. The cook and the dishwasher stand between me and the doorway.

I'll be out in a second.

Sure, I say.

He ambles towards the main room. Not wanting to be in this room alone with the Mexicans, I bow my head to avoid their eyes and hurry towards the back door. Their eyes feel as strong as desert sunlight through my shirt back.

The air feels fresh against my face but beneath my legs the dark asphalt is hot like an oventop, even through my jeans cuffs. Car metal bathed in sunlight clicks and snaps. As I walk past the cars I wonder if I am being followed but do not dare turn around. Ahead, there's a sliver of shade thrown against the stucco wall by a protruding rain gutter, and I move towards it and then lean against the wall.

In the corner of my vision the cook and dishwasher

linger in the doorway as I look across the highway towards a dark grove of bow-legged trees. Beside me the shaded paint feels cool through my shirt, and I lean my cheek against the coolness and it is then that I feel them coming. It takes them a minute.

Yo, one mumbles.

It is just like Tomas and his friends all over.

Yo, you hear me?

I turn. The youngest one, who is maybe seventeen but taller, nods at me and slips against the wall, leaning a shoulder in. His skinny friend with hunched shoulders and hands shoved in his pockets trails him, like a little magnet.

What is it?

The tall one nods at me, What's your name?

The tow truck guy told you.

I forget.

Gabe.

The other one snickers. It's possible the bigger one meant something funny, or just that the little one is nervous and laughs at whatever his friend says. It is hard to feel them out clearly, which maybe means I am too edgy.

Yeah Gabe, nice to meet you.

He puts out his hand. I look at it and hesitate, but shake it. His skin feels clammy, and his grip is loose.

So what you doing around here?

My car broke down, I say. Like the guy told you.

Yeah.

Sure, the other one says.

His leader peers across the lot towards the back door. Is the big guy your friend?

I shrug.

He's just towing my truck.

They trade glances. So he's not your friend? the big one says.

I just met him.

Because you seemed really friendly.

He scratches the pimple on his chin. I try to think of something to say. A sparrow perches on the leafless bough, perched on its claws. Against the sky it appears as a black silhouette.

Hey. Who do you run with? the little Mexican says.

Shut up, the big one says, nudging him. He gestures for his friend to wait, holding his hand out flat. The little one frowns, looking at his shifting feet.

Run with?

I think you know what he means.

Nobody, I tell him.

He studies me.

So then what about your car?

It isn't mine.

You *steal* it? he says, eyes widening, as if he might be in the presence of someone supremely stupid.

No I didn't steal it.

What then?

It's my brother's.

Some kind of a brother you have.

What do you mean by that?

Let you drive a car like that. Could be dangerous.

Finding no words, I shrug and look away, which is difficult since he stands so close I can feel his hot breath in my face. These guys are from little small-town gangs at best. There is no way any of them would deal up here because the wetback cowboys would kill them. They are nothing.

Nada. But they know they have me here alone and you can feel their excitement at the novelty of me. They want to make a bigger deal about this than anyone from back home—from a real city—would bother about. Like a short man with a stiletto, annoying yet dangerous. I try to glance over at the back door, but Stone is not there. All I can see are some chrome pots hanging from the ceiling inside.

Where you taking it to? he says.

I gotta go, I say, stepping aside.

They tense, stepping towards me. The wall is behind me and in my jeans pocket my ice pick seems to announce itself. Maybe I should lower my right hand toward it, but they could notice. It is hard, but I keep my hand in front of me, a knuckle pressed against my belt buckle.

What's the hurry?

I told the tow truck guy I'd meet him by his truck.

Stone?

Yeah.

He has a name, he says.

I don't answer him.

He know you're Mexican?

I ain't no Mexican.

What do you mean by that?

Nothing.

We say nothing. They do not look at each other, though something is going on between them. The leader eases his hand lower by his back pocket. In the high dark branches of the leafless tree yellow blossoms perch like brilliant algae. All birds have stopped their chirping and it is deadly quiet. No sound on the highway. In the restaurant no sound, nor in this parking lot. Something about the heat. The time of day.

My hand muscles twitch. About my temples beats a nauseating pulse and a glitter of sunlight flashes up in the roof gutter and blinds me to a dark bird fluttering past.

Then Stone's voice calls from the doorway.

The cook and the dishwasher back away, but the big one keeps his eyes on me. It is like I have no skin and he is looking inside me. Now that words do not need to come, it is easier to hold his stare. The little one looks at the ground, giggling at himself, while the big one mad-dogs me. He doesn't even turn around as they pass Stone and return to the kitchen, then he lingers in the doorway, still eyeing me.

My guess would have been that Stone wouldn't notice, but he senses something and turns to the big one and tells him by name to cut it out. He swats his hand at the space before their eyes, as if he could cut up the feeling or disperse it. The boy takes a step backwards, but Stone lunges forward and holds up a palm. Rattled, the boy retreats to the kitchen and I realize now that they are only small-town boys, poseurs, although there were two of them and only one of me and probably they had more to prove. Or maybe they were just bored and curious and wanted to sniff me out.

Suddenly Stone actually shoves the little one after his friend. They seem as surprised as I am.

What you do that for, Stone? the big one says, sounding hurt but standing his ground in the doorway.

You want to mess with my customers?

We were just talking.

You want me to tell Susan and she'll tell your mother. Big man.

I don't care.

Get back inside.

You think I give a shit? he says, but backs inside. Stone

102

looks angrily after him with his chin outstretched and his cheeks red until the boys' feet back clearly beyond the threshold. Stone's hand is open like a board and even from this distance you can see that his nostrils are flared.

The boys mumble but disappear.

Satisfied, he turns and ambles towards me. He sits on the hood of an old blue Chrysler to catch his breath, crinkling the metal, and lets his chin double up as his head sags forward towards his chest. The back of his arm comes up to wipe his forehead.

Hope they didn't rattle you too bad, Gabe.

No problem, I say.

Sorry about that.

I wave with my hand to indicate that it is nothing, nada. It is an awkward ghost of a gesture I have seen Tomas use adroitly many times. Immediately I am sorry I used it, but he does not seem to notice it is not an Anglo movement.

He half smiles upon me, father-like, then pats my shoulder. Damned spics, he says almost gently.

As he shakes his head, I look away and nod, and then we walk to the cab. He complains and for a minute I think he speaks of the boys, but then realize he means the old guys who looked away from him inside. They do not understand the urgency of our situation. They have not lived in Los Angeles like him and me. They think they have the *luxury*. He is the one with the engineering degree. The sorrow. He sadly shakes his head.

I would like to voice agreement with him, but I do not. We sit for a few minutes in the hot, stale air as he contemplates the empty field which spreads out before him. Hot air rises from the hood and blurs the horizon. I would like to roll down the window but do not. He does not seem to notice how quiet I am, or how still my hands are in my lap. Finally he reaches below the wheel and starts the truck and we pull out onto the faded highway then enter the cool shady timber of the woods that lead to Oregon.

V

We pass the state line from California into Oregon. The road sign is so faded and weathered by the sun you can barely tell it was once green. I can hardly make out the faint word *Oregon*.

With him now focused on the road, I relax and notice more about him. His shirt is damp and dark at his breasts and underarms and also now along his sides. Each time we emerge into a clearing and sunlight peeks below the window's top edge, it catches his face, which glistens with sweat. Lit like that, his eyes appear amber and warm even when he squints. My father's were light like that—or I should say they are. He is alive, but I can barely remember him.

We enter fields of light green that glow in the afternoon and meadows of yellow flowers. Once again sprinklers feed crops with spray that billows upward in the shape of silver umbrellas, catching the sunshine. We enter woods again and pass a logging rig, its platform loaded with great timbers cut and stacked. In its wake dry needles scatter and settle upon our windshield. The dirty glass glows in the flickering sunlight. Stone turns on the wipers to push off the dust.

He seems rattled and after half an hour we pull over beside a meadow and he reaches back and pulls out two beers and offers me one and he pulls out two folding chairs and sets them on the cab top. We sit in the sunlight, eyes closed but warm, smelling the grass and pollen and pine needles. Even through my socks the roof metal feels warm. A semi passes and the wind ruffles our clothes and vibrates the cab roof but it settles and remains quiet for some time. He senses that I do not like the taste of the beer and laughs, and lets me grab another root beer. It goes easily down my throat.

It reminds me of when Tomas and I were little and my father would bring us to the highway that runs along LAX to sit on his Corvette hood and watch the underbellies of landing planes. The metal glinting against the sky. The white sliver of beach to the west, before the ocean, and the thunderous crack of jets and waves. That was before Tomas had found any Mexican friends, and we had run down the highway looking for rocks to take to the beach and skip over the water.

Chapter three

I

On the drive into Meridan, Oregon, Stone seems quieter, more pensive. We round a hilltop of drier, thinner pine trees and descend into the city valley. Though from above it looks like a small city, once we reach the flats the highway turns into a suburban street. We drive beneath traffic lights and alongside us strip malls quickly pass. There is no traffic on this Fourth of July weekend, the parking lots standing empty, and we progress rapidly towards the downtown without seeing an open service station.

The man does not say anything, though he must be wondering where I am going to leave my car. In Los Angeles you would find someplace open on any day of the year except maybe Christmas, but this is not LA and as we drive onto the downtown's wide one-way street we no longer see even the closed service stations of the suburbs with their shuttered garage doors. I do not know what to do. He must be waiting for me to say something about where to leave the car so he can get back home. Now that we are inside the city limits it feels like every inch this man drives is an act of charity for me.

Don't look so pale, he says.

Do I look pale?

Maybe.

He grins and taps at the steering wheel, clicking it. His fingernails are black with dirt crescents at the ends.

You could drop me off anywhere, I say.

You mean on one of these empty streets? he asks, as if I have said something ridiculous.

Sure.

Don't be crazy.

We drive on. The sun has lowered into the nest of pine trees on the valley's far ridge top. Yellow light comes through in broken rays.

So it looks like all the stations are closed, he says.

I guess so.

You had any place in mind where you wanted to put the car?

I shake my head.

He nods to himself. I see.

If you pulled over at a pay phone I could take a look at a phone book, I say, trying to keep my voice from breaking. Maybe I could get an idea that way.

He purses his lips and ponders over this. Problem is they stopped putting phone books in pay phones because people kept ripping them out.

Really?

Sure.

For a moment I take this in.

You mean even here? I say weakly.

Even here.

The truck jerks over a pothole, clattering something against the cab back, a thump behind my seat, then lifts me for a moment off the vinyl and then we round a corner and my weight shifts against the door and the plastic handle presses into my arm.

He seems to be waiting for me to say something. The sky has gone from afternoon blue to early evening orange, as if a fire burned on the far side of the west bordering mountains. A scent reaches my nostrils that smells like ash but it is probably my imagination and only pollen or pine or city soot.

He comes to the suburbs and loops back towards downtown. He says nothing. It is as if this were a normal action. We pass some car dealers, their cars in ordered and abandoned rows. All places I have seen before, nowhere to put my car.

I look out the window, scrunching my eyes so they will not tear.

From the corner of my vision I feel his measured glance. Familiar storefronts pass on either side.

I tell him: Do you think if I left the car in front of a station somebody might steal it?

For a moment he seems to ponder this, then finally shakes his head.

Let's just pick one then.

We pass one and another and another, but none feel right. He does not press me to make a choice.

None of them feel right, I say.

I know what you mean.

We near another one with dirty windows and a crowd of old cars stuffed haphazardly into the lot before it. Maybe they would be too busy on Monday and would not appreciate finding a stranger's car there unannounced. Or maybe they would love it, and charge me whatever they wanted to. I can imagine myself walking up to them in the morning with my car parked like that, looking like an idiot. But that is tomorrow.

What about this place? I say.

Could be.

But do you think it would be okay with them to leave it here?

Are you kidding? Of course. They'd be thrilled to find a car here tomorrow morning because then they could charge you all they wanted to.

To this I am quiet.

I tell you what, he says. Why don't you let me leave you in a motel with your car there and then you can call around for quotes in the morning and have it towed someplace courtesy of the auto club.

Sure.

Immediately he turns onto a side road and we ride past some old clapboard houses with lawns and shade and faded yellow grass. He turns into an alley, coming behind some low buildings, barely missing a rusted gutter pipe. He seems confident now of where we are going. We cross three more side streets and then veer into the parking lot of a motel from the rear and it occurs to me that he knows this place well and probably planned to bring me here all along.

You coming in? he says, halfway out the truck door and fingering shut the lock.

He leads me into the office.

After he rings the bell a door opens. A man comes out from a room flickering with television light that illuminates an old plaid couch deep inside. He closes the door behind him and steps beneath the fluorescent lights. The light gives his hand a ghostly color as he gets out a registration card.

Before I can reach for it, the tow truck man begins filling the card out. This seems strange, but I just stand quietly as he finishes. I am nervous because although I have the cash from selling Buster, I have no credit card, and in these places they usually want some sort of an imprint for a deposit. My hand slips into my pocket and fingers the lump of bills and I try to think of what to say. But Stone finishes the card and slips it back to the motel man, who clatters a key onto the table and slides it over to Stone, who then turns from the desk. The hotel man does not ask for any money and remains there watching us.

Okay, buddy, Stone says.

I do not move. He hesitates, looking at me.

Don't look so pale, buddy.

What about a deposit? I say.

Don't worry about that.

But I think the hotel guy forgot about it, I tell him.

A twitch of concern passes over his face, and he eases between me and the man, obscuring the man's face with a shoulder.

It's okay, Stone says.

The man's expression is hidden, and I step sideways to see him. He has started towards the doorway to his living room or whatever it is, but in turning catches my eyes. He pauses. He calls out to me. Stone stands there wanting me to be quiet but the man's head is turned now and I manage to say that he forgot to ask me for a deposit. My hands ease into my pockets to keep from trembling.

The man stares at me. No, you already paid, he says.

No I didn't.

He laughs. You did too, though if you want to pay twice I won't object.

But I didn't.

Come on, Stone says. Let's go.

The hotel guy gestures towards Stone. *He* paid, son.

Stone looks at me shyly. There is something nervous in his eyes.

Why did you pay for me?

No reason.

No, you paid for lunch. I can't let you pay for my room too. My voice trembles from upset just getting the words out.

Don't worry about it, buddy. My treat.

By now the hotel guy is looking at Stone and you can sense that Stone feels this and wants me to be quiet and can we get out of here and so I keep quiet, even though the words want to burst out.

You folks father and son? the man says to me, stepping forward.

He's my nephew, Stone says.

The man regards him suspiciously, but I nod and he watches us as we push open the glass door. We stand beneath the arch of the covered drive and the hotel guy watches us through the window, making Stone uncomfortable, but I stay here anyway. Instead of going back into the inner room, the hotel man takes a seat behind the front counter, facing us as he opens a ledger and goes over it with a pen.

Stone seems impatient to go.

So why'd you pay for my hotel room? I ask him.

Do I have to have a reason? he says, trying to make himself angry but failing.

He tries to pat my shoulder, but only manages an awkward slap, and I do not respond.

Let's just get some of your bags from your car into your room, he says. After a moment he adds: Come on, buddy, don't look at me like that. What the hell do you think this is about?

This makes me blush and look down. We walk to the truck and climb up the platform and open the car door, slanted as it sits, and grab two duffel bags and lug them across the parking lot towards my room. Stone holds the key in his hand, clattering against his leg. But before we get within ten yards of the door, I set down my bag and stop. I cross my arms.

He sighs. Okay listen, buddy, he says. I'm not paying for your room.

The first chilly gust of evening wind blows behind me, parting my hair above the back of my neck, like icy fingers against my scalp.

What do you mean?

I wanted to surprise you.

His meaning does not make itself clear to me. I look at him and wait for more.

Your mother's paying for it, he says.

The sun beats against the white walls of the motel and against the stark plaster of the stairway. In my temples a steady pulse throbs. In the middle of the parking lot the fenced pool is empty but the sound of a lawn chair leg scraping concrete comes to my ears, and I catch sight of a young couple pulling lawn chairs beside it and removing from a paper grocery bag some beers.

What do you mean? I say.

She's here.

You mean my *mom*?

He nods.

This makes me very still. My muscles stiffen in my arms and in my back and the twitching returns to my hand. The boy says something that makes the girl giggle and it echoes in the parking lot, among the motel buildings which surround us.

You've met my mom? I say.

He fingers the shirt cloth at his chest, looking unsure.

He shakes his head.

My temples throb. My mother's brother Betino looks white—they both have Spanish blood—but my mother appears really dark—very Filipino—even though she avoids the sun. I can't imagine Stone meeting her and mistaking her for being white.

Why would she be here? I manage to mumble.

I called your house at the gas station and she was going to fly up, he says. I'm sorry, buddy, but you just didn't look old enough to be out on your own like that. I got your number through your Triple A card. I hope you don't mind. I thought you probably ran away from home.

He waits for me to say something. On the eastern rim of the valley a golden glow bathes the mountaintops, like a fragile crown floating above shadowy foothills. Beyond it a crescent moon is beginning to come out, grinning in the still blue sky.

So are you going to meet her? I say, realizing immediately how strange this question sounds but wanting him to get into his truck and leave. He looks at me strangely.

I don't even know if she's here yet, he says. Hey, why don't we get inside, all right?

He peers down at my bag, then picks it up. Finally I grip the other one and follow him to the door. The curtain in the front window is partially opened and no movement is apparent inside, although she could be in the bathroom or on the edge of the bed closest to the television set, blocked from view. At this point I expect him to knock but he pauses, then turns my way. He asks if I am worried she will be mad at me, and I say no and he nods.

He steps aside and gestures for me to knock. It is understood that she must be inside. He does not know what she looks like, that is clear now, and there must be some way to get him to get back into his truck and leave, but the method does not reveal itself to me.

The wood feels hard against my knuckles. We get no answer.

Stepping up, he fits the key into the doorknob. If I am lucky their flight will be delayed and we will have some time and maybe this man will get into his truck and leave. But the door opens and he steps inside, and even before he turns on the light I smell her scent—then the lamp is on and there is her black suitcase on the bed, opened.

The room is empty.

While the man splashes water on his face over the bathroom sink, I hover by the doorway trying to think of a way to get rid of him before Mom gets back. Hopefully when he gets freshened up he will decide to drive home. Maybe I could even suggest it. It is getting late, after all. But when he comes out I am too embarrassed to say anything and he makes no effort to leave. Maybe he even feels responsible for me.

He calls the front desk and tells me she walked to Denny's to eat. He tells me to pull a jacket out of my suitcase because we are going to walk over and meet them.

II

Now in addition to everything else, as if to make matters worse, I begin to feel embarrassed about the things I thought about him and that he knows I thought them, and so I am shy and keep a few feet back as I follow this man across the parking lot. The sky has faded from evening blue to purple night, and a cool brittle breeze teases my hair.

The Denny's stands across the parking lot, brightly lit from within. As we near I can see in a booth inside the wall-high windows my mother eating with my aunt. Even beneath the light Mom's face appears dark as a shadow—worse than I remembered—and she wears the enormous glasses I hate. Aunt Jessica's presence surprises me. She is my father's half sister, a very pale woman of correct posture who has more to do with us than my father, and who refuses to speak to him on our account, and who seems to have taken Mom under her wing. They are a strange pair to spend time together: Mom, who is Catholic, and Aunt Jessica, who calls herself a feminist and who runs a small chain of lingerie boutiques on the Westside for rich people and celebrities.

As we get closer, the man asks me if I see my mother. I have no choice but to point out their booth.

He nods approvingly, focusing his gaze on Aunt Jessica with her silk blue scarf wrapped stylishly about her neck.

That is some lady, he says, and turns to Mom. But who is that with her?

We stand not fifteen yards away, although neither of them sees us. The room's crowded with old people and a couple of families and a booth of smoking teenagers and a long counter behind which you can see the kitchen. It is a clean room, brightly lit, and my aunt fingers her scarf at her neck. It shines an orchid blue against her pale complexion. My mother nods at something she says and it occurs to me that she is a short woman and that my aunt does all the talking. Mom nods at whatever she says. In response to Aunt Jessica's questioning, she prepares to make an answer, but a waitress comes and Mom sits quietly while the woman takes away their plates.

That's our maid, I say, gesturing towards Mom.

He puckers his lips and whistles in admiration. Somewhere in the empty city a semi roars as if on an open highway, its sound coming to me distantly and echoing through the treeless buildings and crossing the empty highway. He starts towards the door and makes it twenty feet away from me before he realizes I am not following him and he turns and appears exasperated by my behavior and he asks me what is the matter.

My brain scrambles for something to say and finds nothing, but fortunately Mom rises from her booth, clutching her purse cautiously as she begins making her way towards the bathroom. Without a word I follow him.

He shakes his head in bewilderment but opens the door for me without a word and then we enter the warm interior.

Light floods everything. It is a room of bright carpet and no shadow and the sound of clattering trays. Aunt Jessica brightens at our approach. Being formal and stiff from her mother's German side of the family, she does not rise to embrace me, but you can tell she is glad to see me and her rebuke is only mild and teasing.

Well if it isn't the bad boy himself, she says. I'd spank you if you weren't so old. It seems like nobody else in this family has the spine to.

She blows cigarette smoke over her shoulder. A year ago she might have reached over and pinched my cheek, an alarming habit to witness in an upright lady like her, and although now she keeps back you can tell she feels the impulse. She blames my mother's softheartedness for Tomas's behavior, and now mine, and has decided to latch herself onto my mother to get us better disciplined, though she complains that since she is not our mother it is nearly impossible and anyway she sees me as a different and more delicate case than Tomas.

So go ahead and sit down, she says, patting the seat beside her.

Her gesture must seem strangely formal to Stone, who has been standing aside, not sure where he fits in this conversation.

She notices him for the first time, and they exchange greetings. Then she invites him to sit opposite us.

If only he would leave. Sometimes if you will a thought hard enough it will happen; but not now. She thanks him for showing such concern for me. My heart sinks when she offers to buy him dinner, waving a waitress over for a menu before he can either accept or decline.

My head crumbles into my shoulders and I peer into my folded hands.

It's late, I say. Maybe he has to get home soon.

This sounds rude, I can tell, and both of them stare at me. With my eyes closed now I can feel the room's noise vibrating in the table—the people talking and laughing and the plates and silverware and even distinct clattering from the open kitchen.

Don't talk silly, Gabe, she says dismissively. The man has to eat. Besides he's going to get a nice tip. She looks away to blow a curl of smoke that glows in the fluorescent light.

Stone looks down at his fingers, blushing, and he fumbles a few weak words of protest. Despite her refinement, my aunt was trained as a lawyer and she can be impatient with social niceties and sometimes speaks very bluntly. My cheeks burn.

At any time Mom could be back. I look over my shoulder once or twice, towards the hall that leads to the phones and rest rooms, but she is not in sight.

Don't worry, my aunt says, assuming I am impatient for Mom to return. She'll be back soon.

Stone listens to this and it must seem strange to him that I would be so restless to see a maid, but he keeps quiet. His elbows rest on the table and he does not seem to know what to do with his hands.

Fine, I say abruptly. Maybe now we can order dessert.

Dessert? she says.

I begin signaling for the waitress. I'll get her to bring apple pie, I say. What about you, Stone?

Don't be ridiculous, Aunt Jessica says. You haven't even eaten a proper meal yet.

We didn't eat *that* long ago, I tell her.

She looks embarrassedly towards Stone, a gesture meant for me, to tell me to stop. You should only speak for yourself, Gabe.

It's okay. He's not hungry.

Stone regards me quizzically and the tendons on the backs of his fingers tense and loosen but he says nothing.

Gabe! Don't be rude. How could you know what he wants to eat anyway?

My hand has been down, but the waitress already saw me gesture for her and she comes over now. She brings out a pad of paper. My aunt gives her an annoyed look.

The waitress asks what we want.

I'll have the apple pie, I tell her.

Aunt Jessica tells her to cross it out and she does and then my aunt tells her to write down a hamburger for me and the waitress takes Stone's order and goes off. My aunt studies me.

What's gotten into you, Gabe?

I shrug, keeping my eyes focused below her chin where she has knotted her delicate scarf, green and blue, around her neck.

We keep quiet for some time. A long hard moment of clattering dishes and a roomful of crowded chatter and the families and old people talking and the booth with the teenage couple. They hold hands.

Mom must be on the pay phone or dealing with her period or something, she's taking so long. My palms push against the table and I start to get up.

Where are you going? Aunt Jessica says.

Nowhere.

I sit. My hands fold on the tabletop but its surface feels hard against my wrist and hand bones and I turn them on their backs but they look funny to me and I put them palms down. They are pale. Finally Aunt Jessica tells me to stop fidgeting. I stop. We sit quietly for a minute and you can feel her annoyance and the awkward nervousness and Stone feels it but probably does not know what it is about, and finally my aunt turns to him and tries to make polite conversation.

He does not tell her about Mexicans or Asians, thank God. It seems to be something he knows not to talk about around a person like her and it occurs to me for the first time that he must have sensed something about me to bring these things up to a stranger. I wonder what it is, this difference: between my aunt and me. Now he is telling her about his tow truck business and our drive, though he leaves out the part about the cook and the dishwasher.

She is very good at talking, my aunt, and he relaxes and smiles boyishly now and this makes me nervous. Sometimes, it seems, moments like this are when people speak more freely. They get careless. He leans forward, arms gently on the table, voice animated. I look to the doorway—towards the cool outside—and notice a white paper cup tumbling ghostly across the lot.

Now I contemplate rising, but then get the idea that if I do Aunt Jessica will tell me not to because my mother will be back soon. But it has been some time now and she will be back soon, telephone or not.

I wait for them to become more engaged in their conversation, studying them carefully. When it seems they have forgotten me, I slide quickly off the seat and begin making my way through the booths. Unfortunately, some people get ahead of me and I have to slow down as my aunt calls after me.

I get to the door.

Outside it is cool now as a dry wind comes off the snow-capped mountains and simple footlights illuminate the manicured plants and cast little yellow halos. Inside the restaurant Aunt Jessica is coming quickly after me.

She enters the glass doorway, silhouetted.

Get in here, she says.

Her tone is so cold and with the way she holds open the door I do not run across the lot but bow my head and walk obediently inside. She closes the door after me.

We stand by the waiting-area seats. Looking towards the table, I can see that Mom has sat down again. Her purse strap is hooked cautiously about her elbow.

Gabe, are you going in now, or am I going to have to ask you again? my aunt says.

I look at her but do not move.

She is really angry now, clutching her elbows the way she does when she gets mad, but then something in my face seems to make her own expression soften.

What *is* it, Gabe? she says.

Nothing.

Come on, Gabe.

I told you. Nothing.

Is there something you're afraid of telling your mother?

If I told her now, she could handle things and Mom would never know. My mother sits at the table talking with the tow truck guy. I study her eyes to see if anything is the matter, but she seems to be enjoying the conversation. When my father left she cried, and when Tomas was arrested she did not eat for five days.

No, I say.

I start towards the door, but my aunt does not move.

Are you sure?

I nod.

She puts a hand out, catching my chest and blocking me. Her fingers are thin—almost bony—and through my shirt I can feel her sharp, manicured nails.

What's happened to you, Gabrielito? she says. I thought you'd put all that nonsense with your brother behind you. You seemed to be changing so much for the better.

I shrug.

I'm really disappointed, you know.

Maybe she is waiting for a reaction, but she does not get one. Her lips are hard and pressed and her gaze fixes steadily on me.

She sighs, then opens the inner glass door. All right then, she says coldly. Go inside.

The indifference of her voice surprises me, but I enter and start towards the booth. Mom's back is to me but the tow truck man's eyes widen, as if concerned that I have been scolded to an unfair degree. His face appears all sympathy.

Mom turns and, in her excitement to stand, knocks over a glass of water. An awkward moment elapses as she senses the man's impulse to reach over and upright it. Then—no doubt remembering that she is a maid—he sits back down. My mother looks flustered as water begins sliding off the table. She fumbles to pry some napkins from the dispenser and tosses them on the mess. Stone blushes as he watches.

Mom's fingers tremble—she wants to turn to me—and finally she stops the flow and steps into the aisle.

She tries to hug me, but seeing Stone's confused face over her shoulder, I stand stiffly.

She seems to feel this and her body hardens, pulling back. As her coarse black hair pulls away from my face I smell her scent, the same shampoo she has always used, and her favorite makeup.

Hi, I say.

Withdrawn now, she acknowledges my name simply and coolly and begins to sit again, but suddenly rushes back to me and pinches my cheek and grabs my ears. I blush.

No questions, she says. Okay?

She must be afraid that I will bolt off and run away again. I nod quickly, and she senses my desire for her to sit, and we do.

For some reason Aunt Jessica does not introduce Mom to the driver, and as we eat our food I feel them observing me. My mother sits next to the tow truck man, and although I saw him chatting with her earlier, his body instinctively turns away from her as his attention focuses on me and Aunt Jessica, the proper family members. I fumble the hamburger in my fingers, forcing myself to take little nibbles that make me feel sick.

Finally Stone tries to break the silence, turning to Aunt Jessica.

So your flight got in on time, Mrs. Sullivan? he says.

Her knife halts in the air, confused.

Oh I'm not Mrs. Sullivan, she says. I'm married. My name's Jacobson.

I see, he says, looking confused but pretending to understand.

They look down at their plates. We eat quietly. Forks click and scrape ceramic. A wrinkle of frustration passes above my aunt's blue eyes.

Wait, she says. That doesn't make sense.

What doesn't? says the man.

That you should think my name's Sullivan just because I'm her sister-in-law.

He stares at her. Why not?

Well because I told you I'm married, Mr. Garret. It's obvious. I'd have a different name from the boy.

The man glances my way.

Of course I know you're married, he says. I mean— unless you were divorced.

A moment of silence passes.

But I don't see how that means you wouldn't be called Mrs. Sullivan, he adds with rising frustration.

My aunt seems to sense that maybe he feels she was questioning his intelligence and she bites her lip. After a time, the man suddenly looks up.

Whose sister are we talking about, anyway?

No, Mr. Garret—sister-*in-law*.

Okay, sure, whatever you say, he says, throwing up his hands in frustration.

My mother gives Aunt Jessica a hard look—mortified that she would give this man who was so nice to me such a hard time. Aunt Jessica returns to her food, rebuked.

The waitress comes and takes away our plates and returns with the desserts, which clatter onto the table.

Aunt Jessica looks up. I'm sorry, Mr. Garret.

Her hands lie flat on the table.

No problem, he says, relaxing now. I sense Mom relaxing too. Outside a car moves into a parking space and its headlights illuminate the window dust, creating a filmy sheet, and light and shadow shifts faintly across our faces, even in this brightly lit room.

But you know, he adds, I still don't know who you're talking about when you say sister.

My aunt wrinkles her brow.

She didn't put whipped cream on my chocolate, I interrupt.

What? Aunt Jessica turns to me in annoyance.

My sundae. It sucks without whipped cream.

She ignores me, turning back to him. I'm afraid I'm not getting you.

Waitress! I say.

Will you just *sit*, Gabe, she says.

I sit. She starts to say something to the man, but the waitress comes. My aunt holds her words—flustered—and starts to wave the woman off, then sensing my mother watching her, she changes her mind and sends my sundae off for the whipped cream.

What do you say, Gabe? Mom says.

What?

What do you tell your Aunt Jessica?

Thank you.

I look down at my hands. Across the table Stone keeps very quiet. My mother smiles to herself, pleased.

Aunt Jessica seems to forget what she had to say, and we all wait for the waitress to return. About five minutes later she comes back and sets down my sundae. A mound of whipped cream has dropped off to one side, and you can see the ice cream has melted.

Take this back, Mom says.

The waitress turns to her.

What?

It's melted.

It's okay, I say.

No, take it back.

The waitress makes a face but picks the sundae up and leaves. Her pocket rag whips across her thighs as she steps around a corner, finger flicking a strand of hair over her shoulder.

Stone turns to Aunt Jessica.

I'm sorry, he says, but I don't think I'm understanding. You're not the boy's mother?

A silence.

She looks at him. Well—no.

But—

I'm his mother's *sister-in-law*.

I see, he says, looking down at his hands.

The table is quiet.

After a moment of brooding he abruptly laughs. Oh, I see. I guess she couldn't make it then.

Who?

His mother.

Aunt Jessica reddens. Mom nervously fingers her earring. It has happened before that people assumed I was white and that Mom was not my mother.

I can tell that both Mom and Aunt Jessica would like to not have to say anything to this man, but Aunt Jessica feels an obligation to in front of my mother, and forces herself to speak. It is obvious she knows Mom would rather she keep quiet, so it is a mystery to me why she would feel a necessity to talk.

Well no, Mr. Garret, she *has* made it here.

He pauses. I don't understand, he says.

My mother's head is lowered. She looks into her hands.

Well *she's* Gabe's mother—*she's* Mrs. Sullivan.

Stone turns to my mother and regards her and his expression betrays the fact that this possibility had not occurred to him before.

But—

What, Mr. Garret?

Never mind.

No, what?

He stares at me and I look down. Mom sits there beside him. Suddenly his neck and cheeks turn red.

What? Aunt Jessica says.

I can tell he wants to say that I told him Mom was our maid, but is too embarrassed. He shakes his head. My eyes fix on my knuckles. Getting no answer from him, Aunt Jessica turns to her food and we finish in silence.

III

As we leave the restaurant he lingers by the cash register with Aunt Jessica but she seems to insist on paying. Then I am left alone with him in the waiting space before the doors. He leans without a word against some newspaper vending machines. You could cut a cloth with the thin blade of feeling between us. I look at him, his hot glance meeting mine.

Why didn't you tell me, Gabe?

I shrug, looking down.

No, Gabe, you *tell* me—*why?*

My eyes fix on a stack of free local papers, the headlines and words a confusing blur. He studies me curiously.

Why?

He leads the way to his truck and Aunt Jessica pulls out some bills for his tip and he tries to refuse, but it is a feeble gesture, and she gives it to him and he does not look at me as he starts the engine and drives away. He had been polite to my mother and even given her a key chain with a little leather boot dangling from it, but he had no more words for me. We do not wait to watch the truck turn onto the road. We do not wave. It is ten o'clock and he will get home past midnight, but my aunt and mother do not mention this and we walk quietly back to the room.

Aunt Jessica takes the ice bucket and steps outside.

Mom sits on the unmade bed, beside her suitcase.

As I pick up her suitcase and lug it onto the dresser and begin to unpack her clothes and carefully fold her panties and blouses and pants, I try to talk to her, but she is quiet. I tell her about the towns I passed through and Navarro, California. The winged Mobil horse and boys in cowboy boots. The sands that blew in from the desert and covered the faded highway like silver sheets. In her brown palm rests the little leather boot and her wrists are limp and her shoulders drawn forward over her knees.

I ask her if she wants to watch a movie on cable.

What did you tell him about me? she suddenly says.

Tell who?

The tow truck man.

I pause. Nothing.

She shakes her head, disappointedly.

I don't know what you're talking about, I add.

Yes you do, Gabe. Her fingers cup each other, trying to keep still in her lap.

I guess he just assumed, I say, glancing aside.

No, Gabe. I don't think so.˙

Through the walls comes the muffled sound of our neighbor's television set. I slam shut her suitcase.

Okay, fine, don't believe me.

Why was he ignoring me?

I don't know. Some people can be rude, I've noticed.

Gabe.

What? I face her, the blood violent in my fists.

Gabe.

I already asked you—*what?*

Did you tell him I was your maid? she says.

I am silent. She studies my face, and the motel curtains catch the headlights of some car in the parking lot.

Of course not.

She looks down, shaking her head. That's what he told your Aunt Jessica.

She must've got it wrong.

He told her you told him I was your maid.

Then he's lying, I say. I stand in the corner now, the wall close to my back. From the muffled TV noises you can tell it is drywall and hollow. The dim lamp throws a shadow over the lower half of my body.

A maid.

I thought I told you he was lying.

Why would he lie, Gabe?

When did he supposedly tell her? He wouldn't have gotten the chance.

He told her by the register, she says.

He didn't have the chance.

Yes he did.

I tell her it is a lie and he was never near my aunt and did not say anything. I add that if she does not want to believe me, then I am sorry she found me. Mom sits very quietly. The more quiet she is, the quicker my words come, and they spill upon me like vomit, my jeans, my face, the walls, the floor. It is dark, this room, and I am talking and thinking and believing that maybe she believes me.

Then the words stop coming.

I am still angry at her when she begins to cry, softly.

I hesitate. I step towards her.

Mom?

She does not move. Her head is lowered and I can only see the top of her crown, the matted hair. For the first time I notice her hair roots are gray. I want to reach out but do not know how. Finally I sit timidly on the bed beside her. My arm just barely touches hers. Still, she doesn't move.

Mom?

I lift my arm and wrap it awkwardly over her shoulder, and though she does not pull back, neither does she respond. I let it stay there for a moment, limp like a fish.

Please don't cry.

Now she does shrug my arm off and I jerk it back as if it had been hurting her. We sit not touching and I want to do something, but she will not let me.

Then a key scrapes in the door lock and it opens, and Aunt Jessica comes into the doorway clutching the ice bucket and three cans of cold soda, and in the crook of her elbow is a Milky Way bar, my favorite. She stops, staring at me.

My mother does not look up.

Without a word Aunt Jessica sets down the ice bucket and the sodas and leaves the room, closing the door behind her.

PART
THREE

Dear Ika,

Enclosed you will find some photos Millie found among Mommy's possessions. They had been packed in boxes in her room which Millie opened as we made renovations in preparation for Malaya's graduation party. Of course I know that it is of some concern to you that we have to clear some of these possessions in order to build a new guest room. This room has been an important remembrance of her final sad months, but we have saved some possessions for you. We found your boys' photos among them and thought you might wish to keep them.

Though I have not looked through all of them, I had occasion to notice some photos of Gabe and Tomas as little boys. It brought back memories of the trips we took to Los Angeles in '85 and '91 and also of the earlier trip you made to Manila in ('83?). In Manila they were such well-dressed, quiet children. Perhaps they seemed a bit shy, but I was impressed by how attached they were to their mommy. Gabe was always by your side, and though initially Tomas also seemed not to want to stray, I recall that eventually he gained the courage to play with his Filipino cousins. Tomas in particular was quite handsome. As I recall, he took to the animals such as the parrots and carabao and wished to start an import business to ship them to Los Angeles. Such ambitious ideas for a nine-year-old! With their mestizo looks they would have been very successful with the girls, no doubt, which perhaps can give quiet boys confidence that will leave them with a serenity allowing greater application to their studies. It is a shame you will not send your boys to live with me in Manila. I could teach

them the values of education, work, discipline, and respect for
their elders and Asian and Spanish heritage.

I can understand why it might be difficult for you to send
your boys away. Parting could be very difficult. But may I suggest
that it is not too late for you to return as well. I have been told by
Lola Cunching, upon her returning from the States last month,
that you made a great insistence of the fact that you have lived
in America longer than the Philippines. Almost as if there were
something wrong with being Filipino! This fetish you seem to have
for being an American seems to me quite disconcerting. Filipinos
have their problems, of course, many problems, but I can assure
you that in fact we have virtues as well. Perhaps some people in
other countries may have a low estimation of Filipinos; may I
suggest that this is inaccurate, a misperception based on seeing
the many poor, uneducated domestic laborers and bar girls who
must live abroad to earn money, as you yourself should well know.

In fact, I am certain you recall a life very different than the one
you might expect to encounter if you were to return. The old
hacienda may still be in ruins, the countryside overrun by commu-
nists, and San Pablo more crowded and dirty than we ever knew it to
be, but my house in Forbes Park has been expanded since you last
visited. Indeed, I might say that the neighborhood generally has
never looked better. There are more diplomats and embassies, the
church has undergone renovations, and we now belong to the Polo
Club, a place you may recall the Americans formerly did not allow
nonwhite Filipinos to join, where you can get a facial and the boys
could go swimming. And though Manila has more traffic and people
than ever, armed guards keep the poor people and crime out.

Millie also found some very old pictures of you and Dina at
the hacienda. Lolo Bien's house was already run down, almost in
ruins, but the porch remained intact and Mommy had fitted you
two in nice dresses. I believe these were boarding school uniforms,

so perhaps you were about to part for the last time. Many of our cousins were there, including some of the rowdier ones such as Bong and Checerida, and there is a photo of all of us, perhaps twenty, in front of the old white chapel. It had no cracks then and, framed by coconut trees, could have been an expensive resort. In one picture you held a rosary that dangled from one hand, and I believe it was the one with beads of silver which Lola gave you before she died, and which you could not be parted from. Everyone remembers the sight of you with those beloved beads in the chapel. We all thought you would become a nun, but instead you became an American! You looked very happy in these pictures, so I hope that the Philippines holds some nice memories for you, no matter that the austerity and dependency of our subsequent years may have provided for you unpleasant memories. Indeed, our country must have seemed a sad and unpromising place to raise children then, and for most Filipinos it is even worse now, but my circumstances have improved.

If you do not act soon it will be too late. Lola Cunching told me that she was surprised to see not only how large your sons are now, but also the manner of their dress. In particular, with some distress did she recall the appearance of Tomas. Apparently he showed up to a party you held for her—an elder—wearing a sleeveless T-shirt that exposed some quite ugly tattoos. Moreover, he also had shaved his head in a manner that apparently the Mexican gangsters enjoy having. Through his T-shirt she could see he had a tattoo of the Virgin Mary. The Virgin Mary! I hardly think his motives were ones of reverence. Perhaps he could have been more considerate, so as to not embarrass your feelings in front of Lola, by wearing a long-sleeved shirt. Lola also informed me that he came to lunch late, did not greet her, and sat in a corner with his girlfriend giggling in a disrespectful manner. Lola also mentioned that Gabe came to this lunch with his brother, in the same car.

It is puzzling to me why Tomas could have turned out this way, impossible for me to reconcile her account with the image I recall of him quietly hugging his mother's leg because he was scared of his large, brown Lola (Lola Maganda). Sometimes I try to understand this. However, I cannot. You have always been a dutiful sister, but quiet and impossible to understand. For me your sons are equally difficult to figure out.

Once again may I urge you to send your boys here. It is not too late to make inquiries into courses at Ateneo for this fall. I look forward to hearing your response.

You and your sons are in our prayers always.

Your brother
Betino

A Dirty Penance

Venice, California
September 1993

Chapter one

I

He drives us through Culver City past glaring strip malls and empty storefronts, the sidewalks so bright they make me squint, and we catch a red light at the car wash on Overland where wetbacks stand in clusters, holding their rags and hoping for tips. They turn and glance in our direction, at my brother's new Explorer, and I avert my eyes.

He takes us along Venice High down towards Abbot Kenny Street. On the threadbare lawn students sit with their backpacks and others lean into cars by the sidewalk and gather in groups by the fence. Hanging out. Next to it stands the apartment complex, with its phone number and orange FOR RENT banner furled across three windows. Little colored flags stick out of the lawn. I am sorry for the poor foreigners who are attracted to the nice building front and do not know what they are getting into. I lasted in Venice High a week until a black kid came running down the hallway, chased by some others onto a playground of bright, weeded concrete and was shot surrounded by a crowd of kids. He died the next day. The black girls were clustered and vicious and I avoided walking by them in the hallways and schoolyard. I'd spend whole breaks in the bathroom waiting for the sounds of feet scurrying into the classrooms to fade, and then I would come out into the empty hall and arrive late for class. I did not last long, but there are people I remember well and would not want to see again. Now, I duck low in Tomas's new truck, but nobody from the school's lawn looks in our direction. We are only a couple blocks from the Venice Hood, but also near Marina Del Rey, and you will find nice condos here among the older, weather-beaten bungalows with the peeling porches and the old black people who like to hang out on them. We get to South Santa Monica. Abbot Kenny Street's New Age boutiques and artist's stores look funky and bright with afternoon shoppers. At night here it is empty except for the black kids who hang out at the liquor store and the Lee Fan kick-boxing students who are not afraid of the black and Mexican gangs that come here to shoot each other and sometimes die.

Tomas hangs a left onto Westchester. The air here smells cool and salty. I catch blue glimpses of ocean between the buildings whose walls are wind-beaten; my brother turns in that direction and we pull into an alleyway between two apartments. It is narrow here, the walls above us chipped and faded by salt and wind, and the buildings stand on metal stilts above unsheltered asphalt crowded with nice cars.

Keep your eye out for his yellow Jeep, he says, not bothering to turn to me.

I sit in back, my fingers in Greta's fur, because Tomas will not let me sit up front any longer. Greta can feel the nervousness in my hands. Beneath my feet lies the tire iron; I am to use it on Eddy Ho's yellow Wrangler. I try to keep my trembling hands calm in her warm fur and concentrate on the cars we pass. They are parked close together, sometimes one behind another, so I have to strain my head to get an angle around the rear vehicle. Often, all I can make out is a glimpse, barely enough to let me know the color of its paint. Beside me, Greta breathes rapidly.

I try not to say anything, but feel sick. I open my window for air, but poke my head out so Tomas will think I am just getting a better view. Our mother thinks he has taken me to a movie. She did not ask me about it. She does not ask me about much anymore. Like always, it is best not to think about how she would feel if we got caught. The first time I went on one of these outings I shook real bad, but after the time we nearly got caught in Bel Air it hit me that she would have found out, and my stomach started twisting up even worse. Each time it gets sharper, and the last couple of times I vomited on the truck's carpet. He got mad and ran a broken beer bottle across my skin. He made me pull off my shirt so he could do it on my chest where our mother would not see the damage he did to my nipple. The scabs are long and thin and hardened, and resemble the course of a dirty teardrop. I force myself not to pick at them. But each time Mom comes home or I start worrying we will get caught and she will find out, I get anxious and catch myself scratching at it through my shirt. When I undress at night flakes fall loose onto my white bedsheets.

Do we really have to do this? I finally say.

He hits the brake and slows. I jerk forward and steady myself and he turns to me. I can't believe you have the nerve to ask me that, Junior.

I make a point of concentrating on the parked cars we drift past. My hand rests on Greta's warm neck.

Sorry.

Man, I can't believe you.

I said I'm sorry.

He shakes his head and speeds up again. At this rate you're gonna still owe me when you're an old man.

The cool air feels blustery in my face and hair. I'm just worried about how Mom would feel if we got caught, I say.

You thought about her feelings real hard when you took away Buster.

I told you I would steal her back for you.

You would steal her back.

Yeah.

He shakes his head.

I *want* to.

I would like to see that one, Junior.

Anyway, it isn't like she was worth all that much, I say, then immediately regret my words.

He looks at me sharply and I face the window again. The apartments move by, some high and modern, though you also get glimpses of the sooty canals and weedy walkways that run between crooked old bungalows hippies lived in during the sixties.

I only meant that I've already stolen a lot for you.

He keeps staring coolly forward. We pass an old aquagreen apartment, and beneath its peeling pastel paint you can make out older, darker layers, and sometimes the worn surfaces of molding wood.

Junior, if you don't stop talking like this I'm gonna wrap a piece of kite string around your neck and pull it tight.

I tighten my lips and pull Greta closer.

After I got back from Oregon, when I still jammed a chair under my doorknob to keep him out at night, he started brooding over how we could steal Buster back from the celebrity. But there was always a maid or gardener or pool man around the house. Plus, the celebrity is too famous for the cops to blow a burglary off. Tomas knows these neighborhoods, places like the Palisades, Beverly Hills, or Bel Air, because many of his dog-owner clients live there. He says most of them leave their side doors open; they tell him to just walk on in. Sometimes he will come upon the kids alone at home smoking pot with their friends.

It kills him that we can't go after Buster, because in some ways it would be so easy—she knows us, would walk right up to us, and since they now have a guard dog they are probably lax about security. But they know Tomas had not wanted to sell her, and when I brought Buster to them alone—early that morning—they must have known Tomas hadn't given me permission, especially when I insisted on taking cash. My brother forced me to go over the words I told them. But finally, he decided if we stole her it would be too obvious that we were the ones who did it.

Later he got the idea that I would pay him back by doing him "favors." Though I have always helped take care of the dogs and to train them, recently he has had me shampoo each of them twice a week, hose down and scrub the concrete cage bottom, and fix their storage shed where the roof is loose and the boards nearly broken. My fingers have become callused and blistered, dried out from so much water and soap. I feed them and wash out their porcelain dishes and walk them and spend a lot of time dog-training for customers. He has a professional dog training service now in which he will retrain dogs people bought from other sources, and his clients include two security services; sometimes they have him go to strange locations for on-site training, like department stores closed for the night, San Pedro shipyards full of imported cars drenched by the cool damp dew of midnight, large warehouses and fenced-in properties the dogs will run around in freely. Sometimes he takes me with him. He charges extra for problem dogs, the biters, the grumps, the touchy and abused and lonely and damaged ones no other trainer would dare handle. My brother is actually great with them. At first I enjoyed seeing the places the dogs guard, but then the fear got tiring, and it leaves me little time for homework.

The more I work, the more he wants me to do. Recently he has said that since I stole from him I should not mind stealing, and since my transgression was a crime, that is what I must do to pay him back. Each time we go out my stomach clutches and I have to step aside and lean over, palming my hands on my knees. I try not to vomit and make Tomas angry, so today I went without food since breakfast.

Now my blood sugar drops and my fingers tremble, though probably that is nervousness too. Beside me Greta's hair feels clumped, my fingers oily. The wind that comes in above the window glass blows damp and cold and throbs like ice in my temples, the way you get after sipping a milk shake too fast. I roll it up. My brother glances my way, annoyed at my movement—which stills me—before he turns forward again. We bound over a deep gutter and the truck bottom scrapes against asphalt, and my brother swears to himself and curses the neighborhood. I begin to hope we will not find Eddy Ho's car and even Greta's breathing relaxes against my arm, but then his yellow Jeep comes into view, parked beneath a rectangular building. Sunlight catches the top story of its crumbling baby blue stucco side.

I don't tell him I see it, but he spots the car and slows down.

Here it is, he says.

I nod.

I can't fucking believe it.

What?

My brother shakes his head. Eddy must be getting soft. He didn't even put on the hard top. He's only got the canvas one on.

It has been cold and rainy today and over the past couple of days, though the sun came out this afternoon. I do not mention to Tomas that Eddy might have taken the top off after the clouds blew out of LA, east toward San Bernardino.

Get yourself ready, he says.

II

The first time I went on one of his trips, my brother picked a place in the Palisades owned by a speculator who buys houses, remodels them, and sells them for a profit. It stood empty whenever the workers left, and Tomas knew a guy who did carpentry work on it, so we knew when they would be gone. No one had even installed an alarm system yet. When we entered, I was surprised: the house had no furniture—just its intricately laid hardwood floors, in octagon patterns, still unsanded. Tomas seemed to know where he was going and went straight upstairs and found a brass sink and we broke up the marble countertop to get it out. The plumbing had not even been hooked up to the chrome faucets, so we took those too. It surprised me he would bother to break into a house just for a sink and faucets, and

I assumed he could sell them for a bundle. But a few days later I went into our mother's bathroom to find some Tylenol, and discovered that he had replaced her grimy old plastic sink with the brass one. In place of the worn plastic faucet knobs he had installed the shiny chrome handles.

I then realized where the new couch had come from, and our mother's new bed that replaced her musty old hand-me-down futon.

On the next trip we singled out an old Hungarian lady's house in Brentwood Park. It was the only house on the block that had no fence or gate, and its lawn sprouted unruly tufts of grass that bent like cowlicks. Apparently, one of my brother's gang buddies delivered drugs for Vincente Pharmacy and brought her her Prozac. She was sixtyish but dressed years younger; her tight dresses and silk robes looked grotesque on her shriveling, suntanned body. She was famous for making passes at delivery boys and house-sitters. Tomas knew she had gone away for the weekend to her Palm Springs condo with her current house-sitter. I thought my brother would go for something like the china or silverware, but he headed for her bedroom. He checked her bathroom and, not finding what he wanted, stood in her bedroom scoping it out. He noticed her vanity—a piece of furniture I had not heard of before—and hurried over to it. On the mahogany surface she had set out a mess of things, including jewelry boxes. But Tomas reached for the perfume bottles and started smelling them and holding them up to the light, as if by looking at the amber liquid he could know which was the most expensive among them, or what would most please our mother. He seemed to know what he was doing, and that seemed strange to me then.

Search the drawers.

What am I looking for?

Find the pearls.

What?

You heard me. Look for the pearls. Or anything with gold on it. Forget the silver stuff. It wouldn't look good on her brown skin.

He was standing there, with his tattoos and shaved head, the cool hard look he'd adopted ever since he got to Saint Dominic's, holding those perfume bottles, and it reminded me of a time we had gone shopping with our mother. This was in Fedco. Back then she used to bring us there, and we loved it. The place was huge. We would run up and down the aisles among the crowds of shoppers, pretending we were pirates in some far-off Caribbean port city. We were friends then. After an hour or so we always grew tired and started searching for her, among all the people, and sometimes this could be difficult. That day it took longer than normal, and I was getting hungry for pizza, which we always got after she paid. I was feeling weak from not eating, and Tomas sensed this, so he had me wait on a chair in the shoe department and searched for her. When he could not find her he came back with a slice for me. He had bought it himself. We finally found her at the makeup counter. She had taken a number— you had to get a ticket and wait for them to call you, because there were so many people—and she was sitting in a chair, practically crying. It turned out they had passed her number without calling it out and she had been too timid to tell them, so she got a new one. I am still not sure why she was so upset—at the time I thought it was all the waiting, but now I suspect she was upset with herself for not speaking up. Tomas put a hand on her shoulder. Then he reached down and uncupped her loosely clenched fingers and took out the old balled-up ticket and brought it to the counter and got a saleswoman's attention and our mother bought the perfume she wanted. Or, anyway, one she could afford.

III

He keeps the motor running. Eddy Ho's Wrangler is less than fifteen yards away, in the open garage.

Don't look so sick, Junior.

I'm not sick.

He studies me. You look like you're about to vomit. You better get outside. If you mess up my upholstery I'm going to add it onto your bill.

I clench my teeth and try to let the angry feeling pass. How many more times are you going to make me do this?

You worry about getting into that Jeep before someone sees us.

You could tell me real quick.

He ignores me and studies the alleyway. A large mutt— unaware of Greta—works an overturned trash can.

Why don't you just tell me now? I say.

Because I don't feel like it, Junior.

I glance at the door to the apartment and also the little door inside the garage right next to the Jeep. Over the last few minutes, riding through the alley, we have seen a lot of people getting out of their cars, returning from work, all potential witnesses. My hand finds the chrome car-door handle, warm and slippery with my sweat. But I hesitate.

Do you really think it was a smart idea to come during daylight? Maybe we could come back after it's dark.

A smile comes across his face. Junior's scared.

Fuck you.

Greta gets nervous beside me and I pet her to calm her as I reach over with my other hand to open the door. I almost stumble as I step onto the crusted asphalt.

He calls back to me. Take it with you.

What?

The tire iron, he says, grinning.

I was *going* to grab it.

Sure.

Wind flaps my shirt and the fabric feels stiff against my skin. I lean into Tomas's Explorer, my ear brushing against Greta's leg fur. The shaft is heavy and cold in my hand and I almost stumble as I back onto the crusted asphalt, trying to keep it out of view by letting it hang by my leg.

I told you I was going to grab it. Can't you listen?

That makes a lot of sense, Junior. It was lying right next to you.

I didn't want to hurt my back.

Yeah, you're so old and have worked so many hours in that suit behind your important desk.

Father Ryan says you should watch out for straining even when you're young. *He* has back problems. *He* doesn't work behind a desk.

Junior, you hang around old people too much.

Yeah, old people like you.

I back off ready for a blow, but he smiles and shakes his head, then goes all cool again and stares down the street and peers up at the apartment's window. You'd better go, man, he says.

Greta stares at me from the front seat, not sure if she should follow, but I do not call and she sits back down. I raise the iron from its hiding place against my leg, its weight straining my arm. Greta watches it carefully.

I cross the alley. My knees are weak. I barely seem to have the energy to keep the rod from falling out of my fingers.

Above I see his lit window—a sliding kind, the type without a pane—crusted white with salt. Like a shower door it is steamed up, so probably they cannot see anything but a blur. I duck into the garage, sheltered from the wind. I peer in the Jeep to check for a red alarm light. Nothing.

I have seen Tomas do this before. He always swings at the front window real quick, so it will smash on the first try, then he gets in and out and we are back in his truck. Alarms do not faze him.

Something rubs against my leg. I jump, but it is only Greta's warm face pushing against my jeans.

Hey, girl, I whisper to her.

Though she seems glad to be near me again, her panting is not as eager as usual. Her eyes are focused, still and alert.

I tell her to stay, and grip the iron tighter, lifting it behind me, pausing, then swing it forward against the glass.

It thumps off and falls from my hand and clatters against the concrete. I freeze—ready for the alarm—but its blaring never comes. Greta starts rapidly pacing, her ears perked. I avoid looking over at Tomas as I bend over to pick up the rod. My trembling fingers, in their hurry, miss it. My nails graze the concrete and it takes me a moment to get a firm hold and finally lift it again. I try to keep calm and not allow Greta to become too excited, but she spots a dog hurrying along the alleyway and goes off sniffing and disappears. I glance at the apartment door, wondering if I should give this up. But with my brother waiting I lift the tire iron to chest level and get ready and decide I have to do it now.

I swing harder. The impact vibrates my bones, but the glass only cracks.

I take it back—in two hands like a baseball bat—and swing again, and this time a few pieces of glass crumble and fall inward. I knock enough glass in to reach through and open the lock.

I find the stash in the glove compartment where Tomas said it would be. I cannot believe it. It does not seem like it should be so easy. I am so relieved I barely bother to unwrap the foil to make sure I have got it, then crumple it shut as I back out.

When I look up the apartment door is open.

I freeze. The doorway is empty. I look around hurriedly and, blocking me from the alleyway, stands Eddy Ho, over six feet tall and half Samoan, in a faded UCLA Law T-shirt. He appears barely more than a silhouette with the daylight behind him, and seems cold and angry. A knife hangs down from his hand. I notice he is squinting to make me out and realize he has not recognized me. In a strange way I start dreading that he will. He was four years ahead of me at Saint Dominic's, though he graduated and takes classes at Santa Monica College now and lives in this apartment his parents bought for him because they still live in Taiwan and want him to get a US citizenship. He lives with his sister, who goes to law school, though they barely talk. Tomas says the parents are Mormons and eventually want to move to Salt Lake City. He is not really a dealer—he only sells to friends—and gets money from his father. I used to watch him play pickup games with some black guys on the basketball court across the street from the church. Although most of the older students did not know who I was, he was still friends with Tomas then, and used to call me Gabrielito and Little Brother.

I can't see my brother behind him, and Eddy senses me

looking and knows I am looking and this seems to give him more confidence. He takes a step forward and I wonder if Tomas is going to leave or help me, but he does not come up behind him.

Then Eddy stops. He leans closer, squinting.

Gabe?

His face starts to relax and he looks bewildered. Immediately I remember the heavy tire iron hanging from my left hand and I try to ease it behind me without drawing his attention. My other hand still clutches the foil, warm and damp and too big to hide in my fist.

Is that Gabrielito Sullivan?

I say nothing.

What the hell are you doing here? he says, beginning to smile, but then notices the foil in my hand. His smile fades and he glances at the broken glass and I can see the gears of his mind working it out. He looks at me. What the fuck do you think you're doing?

I'm sorry.

What the fuck, Gabe, he says, then sees the tire iron dangling behind me. It is all I can do not to drop it.

Look. You can have it back.

You broke my fucking window, he says, shaking his head. You broke my fucking window and you think it's that easy?

I'm sorry.

You're sorry.

I'll fix it.

You think it's that easy? He shakes his head again. You seemed like such a nice kid, Gabe.

Here, have it back, I say, and toss the foil on the ground between us. It tumbles off his shoe. He looks at it and shakes his head, and though I expect him to pick it up, he gently kicks it under the car. His attention never really leaves me.

Suddenly I realize he is serious. I stiffen, not sure if I should threaten with the tire iron or drop it and throw up my hands. I want to toss it and run, but there is no way to get around him to the alleyway.

I hope he might simply be scaring me and will put the knife down. Then he lifts it and starts towards me. I swing the rod backwards but the end seems to catch on something—it hits the car, I think—and my elbow folds awkwardly. He sees this and leaps forward, one arm extending the knife and the other reaching to pin my wrist that holds the iron. My eyes catch the blade flash, then vanish, and I curl back, hiding my face and shoving my shoulder in his direction. I wait to feel the clean stab that will break my skin and stop against my cartilage or bone. It could tear and rip and slice muscle. I stare at the side of the car—not daring to look—but catch a second flash in the side of my vision and the blue sky behind the descending Samoan. For a second I worry he will scar my face, and my eyes shut as if this could stop it.

But then I feel Greta scramble over the Jeep's front hood, and hear her growling fevered barks as she leaps towards him fangs first, eyes bulging, and then the open mouth aimed like a snake fang at his knife arm. His eyes widen—surprised—and he tries to back off and point the knife at her. She catches his forearm and elbow and the weight of her slams him against the neighboring car.

As I stare at him I wonder why he is not screaming or calling for her to stop, and then I realize he cannot. There is a clicking sound, like a coin in a drier, and I realize it is his metal buttons clanking against the car.

I notice his knife lying on the ground and pick it up. I call in German for Greta to stop and she lets his arm go and backs off. She eyes him, growling low and deep, her black lips drawn away from her fangs. One of her eyes is milky with a cataract, which makes her look rabid and evil. Eddy, who has collapsed into sitting, stares at her and hardly notices his mangled arm.

Now I can see over Greta's head. The sun has come out and the daylight nearly blinds me, and my brother stands there over Greta and Eddy. His arms crossed, the stubble on his shaved head giving a rough edge to his silhouette.

I get up and stare down at Eddy.

Let's go, I tell my brother.

Tomas doesn't move. Where's the foil?

What?

The foil.

He does not seem in any hurry to leave. I think it's under the car, I say. Let's just go.

Get it.

I stare at him. *He's* lying in front of it, I say, nodding towards Eddy, who eyes the dog again.

So move him.

He's bleeding.

If you don't lick him you won't get the AIDS.

I shake my head. I'm not touching him.

He picks up the tire iron I dropped. He hands it out towards me. I'm not telling you to touch him, Junior. I want you to beat him out of the way.

I shake my head. Tomas gives me a look but steps towards Eddy and sets the sole of his foot against his shoulder and begins to shove him over but Eddy quickly crawls a foot or two out of the way. My brother reaches under the car and grabs the stash. Then he looks down on Eddy.

You were going to *knife* my brother, he says to him.

No I wasn't.

Eddy, he shakes his head. Don't even try.

My brother has a steel-toed boot. When he descends on him, Eddy is all curled up against the corner, and for a moment I see Eddy's eyes pleading for my help. Then he covers his face. Tomas kicks the back of Eddy's knuckles and they look crooked and broken, bleeding, the skin torn off the thumb. The sound of his boot slapping into Eddy's back and legs sounds like a hammer thumping into raw meat.

IV

We don't talk as we bound over alley gutters, our tires slamming into potholes and the front bumper scraping asphalt. Beside me Greta pants, her tail thumping excitedly against the seat as I hug her. She looks back and forth between Tomas and me, then scrambles to the window and watches people and dogs we pass, then comes back to nuzzle me so I will scratch her face. The fur about her mouth is damp with blood, and a piece of tattered shirt sticks to her gums. But I hug her tight.

On the window she has left red smudges which glow like translucent rose petals clinging to the glass.

Don't look so deflated, Junior.

I'm not deflated.

He gives me a long looking-over.

Okay, sure.

I try to sit up straighter, without letting him notice I am

moving. We pass a black retriever and Greta leaps at the glass, her nails clicking against it like pennies.

Shouldn't we call an ambulance?

He looks at me and shakes his head.

Man, I can't believe you, he says. He was going to *knife* you.

Out on Windward the boulevard's wide, and the buildings low, the sky opened up. Low, enormous clouds move not far above us, and their insides glow with sunlight though the undersides are dark with shadows.

I don't really care about him, I say.

He ignores me. He pulls out the foil and uncrumples it and looks through it and crunches it up and hands it over so I can put it under the carpet. In the past we have often been pulled over, though this has not happened since he got his new car and started wearing straighter clothes (he says too many white kids dress like gangsters now). We pass the Santa Monica cop station, with its ordered rows of police cars parked next to the civic center dome that looks like something out of The Jetsons. I am worried.

V

We come up along Main Street towards the nice part of Santa Monica. Posh stores. Artist's galleries. The pier's archway passes on our left. This is not the quickest way home.

Where we going? I say.

You hungry?

I guess so.

You want Fat Burger or pizza?

My fingertips rest on my jeans. Isn't Mom going to have made something for dinner?

She's working late, he says.

That's not what she told me.

He frowns. You want to eat her tired old paella?

It might hurt her feelings if we eat something else first.

We'll tell her a client made us eat some of her food, he says after thinking a moment. Mom loves it when we do education and work kind of shit.

It sounds like a stupid excuse to me, but my brother seems irritated, so I keep quiet. Lately he has been increasingly inconsiderate towards her. I don't exactly know why. Maybe I notice it more now, after what happened in Oregon. It has been a gradual development, and maybe it has been coming on as Tomas has grown taller and more confident, and found more friends.

At Shakey's we go to the bathroom and splash water over our faces and dab napkins over our face and hands and pat our shirts. The paper comes away damp and pink. I run a few matted napkins through my hair, even though it is so dark you could not see any blood on it anyway. He orders a pizza with lots of meat and pineapples and green peppers, then we go over to the drink bar.

Pitchers of beer are cheap, he says. You want to try it?

No thanks.

He grins. I didn't think so.

He gets me a diet Coke and a beer for himself and we make our way towards a wooden table. I try not to let Mom get into my mind as we watch the game on a TV that hangs from the wall up by the ceiling. After a while my eyes wander and I notice a lady sitting at a table across from us eating her pizza. She is fat, like a Mexican mother, and it seems sad she should have to eat alone. She catches me looking at her and I look away, embarrassed for her, but a few minutes later her kids come up and sit across from her and she cuts them pieces and they start eating off folded paper napkins.

When our pizza comes Tomas cuts me a piece and folds it over the New York way, like he used to, and passes it over on a napkin. We lay out napkins on the wood instead of using plates because that is how we used to do it before Shakey's started supplying dishes and utensils, back when we used to come with Mom. It steams in our faces and we eat the crisp slices on our napkins, though my fingertips can still feel the hot crust through the thin oily paper. The crust is warm and crisp in my mouth as I chew it and swallow. It makes me sicker that it tastes so good. I put my slice down and look up at him. Do you really think Mom didn't cook us dinner?

He shrugs.

I told you. We'll tell her we ate at a client's.

Ever since I can remember, Mom has been making the dishes Dad's mother used to cook, even when we were still living in the Philippines and she had not been to the States yet. Back in the barrio she used to cook a rice dish for her father and brother and something American for Dad. When he was around we ate whatever he did. We were always picking off other people's plates, though, and you could get baked bananas and nuts on the streets and at the markets. Sometimes Tita tells Tomas he should get rid of his girlfriend, who does not get along with Mom, and find a wife who will want to live with her when she gets older, but he does not listen.

In the dark car he glances at me. Don't worry so much, Junior. You can have it for lunch tomorrow.

When we get home the kitchen light is on—she is awake—and I keep behind him as we go up the walk. She is at the counter and the place smells like tomato sauce and baked cheese. The food has been left out. Obviously, she wants us to see it.

She doesn't look at me.

Where have you guys been?

Just kicking about.

I made you dinner.

Oh that's okay, he says. We had pizza at a client's.

A client made you pizza?

He pauses. It was takeout, he says. Anyway, we sort of had to eat it.

She appears not to believe him. He pauses there, uncomfortable for a moment, then walks into the other room, leaving me with her, and it seems too awkward to follow him. She says nothing to me. I think about saying something or taking a piece of the food—though I am not hungry—but I do not and finally she gets up and wraps it and walks past me and goes into the other room.

Chapter two

I

Ever since we got back from Oregon I have not seen too much of Mom. She has always worked sixty hours at a department store's shoe section and recently she has taken a second job looking after an invalid Jewish lady in the Hollywood Hills. The woman believes her dead husband comes back to visit her, after dark, which scares Mom, but she needs the money. She goes there most evenings and does not always come back to cook us dinner. Sometimes she will even stay the night. When she does come home she will wander about the house, and will not say a word or even glance at me. Lately I have taken to walking around the neighborhood on days she is home or during the hours when I think she might get back, so I will not be around for her to ignore me.

On Sunday mornings, though, we go to church together. Tomas used to drive us in the Oldsmobile, but nowadays he refuses to go. He says he is still mad at the priest for kicking him out of Saint Dominic's, though probably he is angry about his car and simply making a point. Sometimes I think about telling him what happened in Oregon—how hard things are on Mom—so he will treat her more considerately, like he used to, but I cannot get myself to do it. When Mom and I go to church without him she sits in the passenger seat while I drive her over in her old Tercel. The trunk has no lock because she did not replace it after somebody broke in, and there is a hole in the floor beneath the accelerator, where wind seeps up around my bare ankles. We go early so she can sit up near the altar, and I do not complain like I used to; when she stays after Mass to pray I no longer point out that she is the only person left, and instead of waiting impatiently outside, I now kneel in the pew next to her.

Sometimes we run into Father Ryan outside, as we emerge from the side doors squinting in the daylight. She will take my arm then and talk to him cheerfully. He is always giving me nice looks because he thinks I am the good one. He never asks about Tomas. Father Ryan is white and pale and from Ohio, but he used to be a missionary in the Philippines, down in Mindanao, then later served as the Chaplain in Forbes Park, so around her he acts like a Filipino, all cheerful and talkative and politely smiling. The first time we ran into him I thought she was in a good mood the way she laughed, but after he went inside, she let go of my arm, and did not say a word on the way home.

II

Today Father Ryan calls me in to talk about my grades.

Gabe, he says. You were always a better student than your brother.

He has discarded the friendly Filipino manner he always adopts with my mother. He watches me behind his wooden desk and the chair beneath me feels hard, its front edge knifing into my legs. His room smells of old wood and dust, like pews, and the chair handles feel worn and oily. His face appears almost like a shadow with the bright window behind him, but you can make out the roughness of his features, made leathery from missionary work done beneath the blazing Philippine sun.

Do you have anything to say for yourself? he says.

This morning I found out I failed a math test, my best subject, which must be why he called me in.

I'm sorry.

I finger my jeans where they fray at my kneecaps, the loose whitewashed strands soft as moss, and try to think of other things. After a while he sighs and pushes a tissue box towards me and then faces away.

I do not take any tissues and turn aside for a moment and keep my eyes wide open. I think very carefully and hard about a pencil sketch he has of a saint on the wall and that seems to work. He senses this, and tosses the box aside.

You used to get good grades, Gabe.

I guess so.

Now you've had a C in English, and a D in religion. And now this F. An F, Gabe. He pauses, as if waiting for me to say something, but I do not. Is there anything you would like to tell me, Gabe?

No.

How are things at home?

Okay.

He studies me.

They are going all right with your brother?

Yeah.

And how is your mother?

She's fine.

And your brother's fine.

Yeah.

He nods to himself, his stiff white collar collapsing under his chin, which he then has to straighten.

And so you are saying there is no problem with your brother at home.

He leans over the desk and sets his arms on the papers piled on it and looks at me carefully. I feel my blood pulsing but I do not glance away. He looks as if he is trying to give me a message like *It's okay:* I can tell him anything and if I just tell him now he won't be mad. Behind him through the window the silver sky burns so brightly it silhouettes a leafless branch right outside the window. Across the courtyard stands the gray abbey, its stone walls streaked below the gutters with black stains that resemble mascara tears. Above its roof the green top of a sycamore glows, ablaze with sunlight.

No, I don't have problems with my brother.

He frowns and looks down at some papers and straightens them and examines a sheet. The times he has been over to the house for family parties he has always been cheerful and talkative and would come over whenever he saw me sitting alone in a corner or in front of the TV, to keep me company. Now, his expression looks very serious.

Then the only explanation I can think of, Gabe, is that you're slipping. You are getting lazy.

I do not tell him I spent three hours last night trying to concentrate on the homework pages. I do not tell him about how my mother and I ate dinner alone last night and did not say a single word. That it is she, not my brother, who is mostly on my mind these days.

I'm sorry, sir.

Don't be sorry with me, Gabe. It's your poor mother who's going to be so disappointed. He shakes his head. You'd think she'd had enough to handle with your brother, but I didn't ever think she'd have to worry about dealing with you.

Sir?

He looks up again.

Yes. Do you have anything to say for yourself, Gabe?

He looks as if he expects me to offer some excuse that he will either have to belittle or accept, but he seems hopeful.

Please don't tell my mom.

He frowns and shakes his head but he thinks for a long moment and then tells me he will call my Aunt Jessica in first and I can go. He says this looking down at his papers and does not look up again and I stand and leave the room.

III

It rained this morning, and drops on the bus window catch the sun like a glowing sheet. Then we round a corner and the sparkling fades and I can see the storefronts again. I study them carefully, trying to calm down. Last night Aunt Jessica told my mother she wanted to see me today at her Montana Avenue store. It will be the first time we have talked since Oregon. I get off the bus. As I walk towards her store my hands jitter, the sidewalk still damp from this morning's rain, littered with dark wet patches that shrink as steam curls off them and glows in the sunlight. There are shoppers here, young people and thin middle-aged women walking with purpose and the crowd of hip-looking people wearing sunglasses at little tables outside the Coffee Bean, studying passersby. I duck my head and hurry past them. Near my aunt's store, I slow: even through the tinted glass I can see the pretty girls who work for her folding clothing as my aunt talks to them from behind the counter. After the girls carry boxes out back, I hold my breath and push the glass doors open.

She does not see me until I am halfway up, and I worry the browsing customers will think I am here to buy something, but they ignore me.

Gabe, she says coldly. Wait out back and I'll get to you in a minute.

She looks back down at her ledger and I go to the backroom where the girls pack boxes and they glance at me but say nothing and I wait quietly by the door. Finally they leave. Some minutes later my aunt comes in.

Come on. Let's go.

The school stands behind a chain-link fence with green canvas that flaps against the wire. The buildings are old houses and warehouses painted pastel colors like light green and baby blue. Aunt Jessica would like me to go here. A weird-looking white sculpture shaped like a roller-coaster rides over the multileveled roofs. It looks like it cost a lot of money. Through a gap in the canvas I can see kids gathered in the parking lot around their cars—many expensive, Jeeps and convertibles, though many of the students dress as if they were from Venice or Compton or Watts.

This is it, Gabe, she says.

We stand on a street so wide it has divider islands of soot-killed grass and parched coral trees. There is an abandoned railroad yard nearby and the freeway overpass has rusted chain-link fences to keep kids from tossing rocks onto cars.

Yeah, I say.

She must sense something weak in my voice because she gives me a hard look. Isn't it good enough for you, Gabe?

I don't tell her what I am really worried about. I keep the corner of my vision on a group of kids sitting on the hood of an orange BMW.

She takes my silence the wrong way. It's a good private school, she says.

I know, I say, but it comes out mumbled and she obviously thinks I do not believe her or care.

Listen. Your mother wants very much for you to go here. It's not cheap. It isn't pocket change for me, you know. You've got to want to do well to make it worth it. She looks aside. Honestly, by your attitude I wouldn't pay for it except that I know how much your mother wants this.

I know, I say weakly.

She looks at me sharply, as if I had said something insolent and she is surprised I would dare to voice it. It's a good thing we got you in before your grades came in this semester, she says. If they ever find out—

She turns and looks up the street and squints and puckers her lips and then she turns back and faces me again.

Look. Gabe. Your mother had hopes when she came to this country. In America you can become successful. You can rise above. You can get education. That's what she was taught by those nuns the American Catholics sent over. My Aunt Jessica frowns, then seems to check herself and takes a breath. But it's too late for her, Gabe. She stops again and hardens her lips and looks down the wide street. Her mind seems to be on some distant thought. She is always hanging out with my mother's younger cousins, who are Filipino nationalists and talk about getting rid of the American bases. They are always talking about white people in Tagalog in front of their faces, even Aunt Jessica, who agrees with them and gives them lingerie. My mother disagrees with them and says they should try to fit in more and should have Tagalog pasted on their foreheads if they love it so much. In the school yard, a bell rings; students jump off the hoods of their cars and clutch their bags, heading inside. Within moments the lot is nearly empty. My aunt's manicured fingertip touches a dusty fence link as she watches and the silent lot seems to make her sad.

Anyway, Gabe, I don't think she hopes for anything for herself anymore. She hopes everything for you. My aunt hesitates. She fingers her frosty blue neck scarf that matches her eyes as if to loosen it, but when her hand comes away the delicate fabric remains tightly knotted around her neck.

And let me tell you something more, Gabe. Your mother has been talking to me. Her brother, Betino—your uncle— has been nagging her to send you and your brother to the Philippines. To stay with him and go to school over there. You know what that place is like—the soot, the crime, the crowds, the people, the kidnappings, the *humidity*? Do you *remember*? How old were you when you came over here— eight, nine? He wants you to live in his house where he can watch over you. And why do you think he's offering to do this, Gabe? Do you think it's because he wants your com- pany? To take you away from your mother? No. He says all this because he believes you are not turning out right, and the reason he thinks that? Well, he talks to your mother, and he can hear in her voice how worried she is. How much it hurts her. Are you listening to me, Gabe? *Gabe?* Do you *understand*? He can hear on a phone from five thousand miles away on a bad connection that your mother is in pain and lonely and disappointed and scared. Behind a curtain of expensive static. You and Tomas are everything to her. You think she has dreams of her own? What, to open up a shoe-making business? To become a millionaire? To remarry or something, go dancing, live it up, have a good time? Like some young, happy-go-lucky single mother? Come on. You know what she's like. She came to this country in the first place, Gabe, even back then, because she had dreams that her kids could have a better life than that caste-driven slum you come from.

Aunt Jessica takes a breath. She lights a cigarette and takes a puff and her heel taps the sidewalk restlessly, as if impatient to stomp a stub out.

Gabe. She's even thinking of taking up his advice and actually sending you there to that humid country where the kids would know each other already and be chattering away in a strange language. That's how worried she is. Would you *enjoy* that? But she doesn't want to do that if she doesn't have to, to live in that country that wasn't kind to her during her childhood, and so I'm trying to get you into Westward.

She glances at the school library, glass and steel modern. Do you have anything to say to me, Gabe?

Her eyes fix on me. I scrape my callused, bitten knuckles against my jeans. I stop myself. Down the street, wind rakes a few withered leaves free from the coral trees and tumbles them across the boulevard and its cars.

It was six years.

What?

I was six years old when I came here.

This stops her. She studies me carefully. The traffic light

changes down the street and a truck shudders past; the smell of its gasoline fills my nose and its soot in my mouth tastes like fine sand. For a moment it seems like she might be concerned about me, might even touch me, because she thinks I am odd, but something changes, and her eyes seek me with hardness again.

What kind of a thing to say is *that*?

I don't know.

You don't know.

I shrug.

Well, *whatever*, Gabrielito. She waves her hand. I don't want you to fuck up. Do you understand me, Gabe?

I nod.

She turns and I follow her with my hands in my pockets. We do not say anything as she leads me to the administration building to take an entrance test.

IV

Sunday comes again and our mother asks Tomas if he will drive us to church. Though I had already gotten her Tercel key and put on my sweatshirt—ready to drive her myself—I keep quiet and hide the chain gently in my pocket.

He turns and looks at her. He wears an undershirt with no sleeves and you can see the gang tattoo in Spanish on his shoulder. It involves barbed wire coiling through a skull's empty eye sockets, and pieces of a shattered cross.

Church? he says sarcastically.

We could go to the ten-thirty Mass.

I'm busy.

She shifts about, flustered. She looks away and then back again.

We could go to the twelve o'clock, she says almost shyly.

He gives her a look.

This evening they have the youth Mass, she adds. You might meet some pretty girls.

Tomas grins, then turns to me. I'll let mama's boy keep you company, he says.

She glances towards me and I blush and look down but she has already turned back to him. In the end, he doesn't come and I drive her to church in the Tercel.

She sits in the front, but over by the far door, clutching her purse that lays between us. She absently regards the stores we pass, a deli, a New Age tea place, a florist shop fronted by white buckets of bright flowers, the Asian man who owns it gathering stems for a young guy who wears an earring and black vest. Mom likes such flowers, and we could pass here on the way back, when I could buy her some for the yellow table vase in the kitchen. I plan to do this. Mass is dim and quiet and afterwards she moves to the pews near the Virgin, lighting a candle at her feet and kneeling before her to pray. I drive her home on a route that will take us by the same flower shop. But as we near, she is faced away, the back of her padded shoulder pointed at me, and stopping at the shop suddenly seems like a foolish idea. I drive us past it without stopping.

Chapter three

I

Lately, he has been leaving me alone, ever since I started doing things to begin paying back for the car and Buster.

He has been especially nice ever since we went down to Eddy Ho's. Since then he has not beaten or picked on me in front of his friends, though if he is in a bad mood at home you have to avoid him because he gets snappy. A couple of times he has even taken me with him to hang out—not just on jobs, like he used to. Twice we went to see some friends who live in their own house in Mar Vista, and once to a girl-friend's Santa Monica apartment. Her mother is only thirty-two and likes to go dancing, so they have the place to themselves most of the time. People hang out there, kids their age—several years older than me—sitting around the living room taking bong hits, watching TV, while couples sit almost on top of each other on the couch. Everyone listens to one another tell stories. Tomas has a friend, Manny, who he went with down to Crenshaw on the second day of the LA riots. They set fire to a house, claims Manny, and passed through a boulevard of burning palm trees. Then they went down to a Price Club and walked out with boxes of new TV sets and stereos. That they went down was news to me. There were older guys in their thirties doing the same thing in Polo shirts, and their girlfriends would be waiting in their Camrys and Acuras. No cops interfered. The atmosphere was so lawless, a camera crew from some local news station was able to film all this without fazing the older guys. Tomas and Manny, though, were too smart to get on film.

My brother has even said he would take me to parties, though for now he avoids them because he wants to wait for Eddy Ho to cool off. He found out a couple of weeks ago that Eddy was alive and not crippled. Somehow his girlfriend heard about it at work. A week ago he heard that some of Eddy's friends were looking for us, especially for Tomas. My brother showed up at a party in Culver City, at one of those modern apartment complexes which are impressive-looking from the outside but whose drywall is so paper-thin you can hear people in the next room breathing and fucking and on Friday or Saturday nights the muffled sound of parties going on throughout the building. Johnny Guerro, one of Eddy's friends, was there and had a few words with Tomas. Luckily Tomas was with some friends, including Manny, who studies Thai boxing and Indonesian stick-fighting with Danny Inosanto, a Flip who teaches Kali in some warehouse in the ratty section of Marina Del Rey, and who was friends with Bruce Lee.

Nowadays Tomas does not let me sit out on the porch. He does not even like me to walk to the local store. Not that I want to. Even when I am at Saint Dominic's waiting for our mother to pick me up, I keep close to the rectory door. I do not take the bus because the bus stop is a block from school, on Wilshire. And I have not gone to the basketball courts across from the church either.

All this time I felt bad that I did not feel worse about Eddy being hurt, that what I mostly worried about was whether his being wounded or crippled would get us in trouble.

Of course I also worried our mother would find out about Eddy Ho. I would study her expression to see if she knew anything, but she did not know anything yet, and still does not. I can tell.

Sometimes at night when I have to go to the bathroom I will pass her room and her door will be open. If there is moonlight I can make her out on the bed. It seems empty by Mom's pillow where Buster used to sleep with her leg hanging off, and at her feet where her cats Saint Elmo and Sister Teresa used to curl up before Buster got to them. Sometimes I think about getting her a couple of new cats for company, but then I become afraid of what she might say when I give them to her, what the cats might remind her of. Sometimes she will be hugging her pillow against her cheek or chest.

Later I will try hard not to think of her there as I try to fall asleep. I also try not to think about the way she looked the day after Oregon. Mostly that day she ignored me. But one time I looked up from my book and caught her looking at me, though immediately she turned away. I only saw her for a second. Even though she looked away so quickly I did not have enough time to tell whether she seemed hurt or angry, still I could not get her face out of my mind. The way she appeared at that moment—it haunts me—and I go over it in my head, trying to figure out what she was feeling. At times she looks mad but at others she seems hurt, and I cannot tell which look is my memory and which is my imagination.

II

The last period bell rings as I hurry out into the courtyard between the rectory and abbey. It is a great asphalt parking lot, covered by black tar so new it shines in the sunlight and smells warm in my nose. The last period bell rings in the classrooms behind me, and I hurry, hearing the crowd of students pouring out of the classrooms. On the front lawn, I wait by a lone sun-withered palm tree, keeping an eye out for my mother, but also a wary one for Eddy Ho's car. Already, the line of waiting vehicles crowds the curb, their hoods dappled by sun that pours through the overhead trees and sifts over the students who sit on the lawn before me.

Then I feel a woman approach, and I clench my bag strap and try to make out who she is without turning and letting her know I see her coming. As if, that way, she might not come.

But by her movements I can tell it is Cynthia Rowe, the biology teacher and orchestra leader. A former dancer, she has a way of moving through people stiffly but gracefully, her hand touching their shoulders in an absent but proper way that conveys some sort of message. I think about going down the block and waiting for my mother there, but it is too late to avoid Cynthia Rowe now.

I used to wait down at the corner because I did not want people to see Mom picking me up. I used to hate how she wears her huge sunglasses, but ever since Oregon I have her pick me up in front of the rectory, like everybody else. Those glasses still bother me, though I try not to think about them.

She will drive up real slow and squint out her window,

looking for me. This is when she does not wear her ugly sunglasses. Even though I could rush up and duck into the car before anyone has had time to see her, I walk up to the car purposefully, casually, stepping around the backpacks and people sitting on the lawn.

Now, I recognize her car, even though it is still half a block away, behind the line of traffic that waits to reach the pickup point. A white Plymouth holds everyone up. Jodi Page takes her time getting into the backseat, and her mother—only her head is visible above the partially rolled-up tinted window—does not seem bothered, and does not hurry her. A few cars back, someone's father waits impatiently, clenching his steering wheel, though he doesn't honk. You are not allowed to get into a car until it reaches the front of the creeping line, so I do not try to walk down the line to my mother.

As she nears, I flinch. She is wearing her bug-eyed sunglasses. She bends forward over the steering wheel, something she needs to do to see the Land Cruiser bumper that is only three feet ahead. When the truck moves forward, she lets a long gap develop (the driver behind her makes an impatient face), then she hits the accelerator and jerks forward, braking abruptly just short of the Land Cruiser. Her Tercel chassis seems to bounce on the stopped wheels.

I begin walking towards her car. My eyes focus ahead and I ignore the clusters of people around me. But my mother's car lurches forward again, and this time she bumps the Land Cruiser. I stop. She hit it hard enough to hear it, and more faces turn in her direction. The mother in the Land Cruiser gets out and walks over to Mom's car. She is blond and tall and thin and wears black yoga-class tights, and holds a Starbucks iced drink.

I step my way around a sitting couple, but halt again. A crowd forms to watch the yoga mother and Mom, who looks confused as the woman leans into her window and angrily talks down at her. My mother nervously pushes her glasses up on her face, listening. I am hoping this will be over soon, when my mother gets out of her car and looks up at her.

Probably everyone wonders who this little Filipino woman is, since she has only recently begun picking me up here. The yoga mom's son, Ben Feinstein, only a few years younger than me, watches from a couple of yards away, looking around self-consciously.

Sweat itches beneath my shirt. I am thinking about what to do when Jordan Hammerson approaches. He had distracted Cynthia Rowe, who then forgot she was on her way over to me.

He comes right up beside me, watching them.

Jesus, she's giving her a hard time, he says.

My mother looks bewildered and she clutches her elbow as the yoga mom continues to talk angrily down at her, one hand on her hip, her other still holding her Starbucks drink. By now the entire lawn of people has drifted over. From somewhere back in the car line someone honks, and others do too.

That's my mom, I say.

Jordan turns to me. Sunlight on his tanned skin creates a golden color, which looks odd against his powder blue eyes.

I know, he says. I've been to your house, remember?

I just wanted to make sure you knew.

He studies me strangely.

Yeah, okay, Gabe.

I leave him and head towards the car. And there is nothing I can do but stand there, close to the yoga mom. Her son, Ben, glances up at me, shifts on his feet, and though he seems embarrassed, fingering his stupid red vest, I'd like to put my ice pick through his cheek. My fingers jitter. I do not know what to do with them. People study me, many of them wondering if I am in a car pool with Mom, though maybe some are putting my features together and figuring out who I am.

Mom is peering up at the yoga mom.

I'm sorry, she says.

The yoga mom's hand is on her slender hip, its bony shape visible beneath her dancer's stretch pants. That doesn't fix my dent, she says. She shakes her head and sighs. Do you realize this is a new car?

Mom tilts her head, like a bedraggled little sparrow. I'm sorry.

The yoga mom ignores her and turns to some random girl standing nearby. I mean, really, some people, she says. I was only a few feet away.

She turns back to my mother. I mean, what were you thinking?

I don't know.

You were only a few feet away.

I know.

The yoga mom stares at her.

You *know*? You *know* and you still *hit* me? God. Can you understand? I'm going to have to bring this truck in, deal with the fucks at the dealership, rental cars. The yoga mom clenches her teeth, her jaw muscles pulling taut beneath skin yellowed from too much suntanning, and she breathes deeply through her nose, a sort of sigh, then opens her mouth again. I'm a busy woman, a *female* producer working in *sexist* Hollywood—I don't have time for this kind of shit.

The yoga mom shakes her head. Well, then you'd better give me your license and insurance carrier.

Mom touches her elbow. I don't have insurance, she says.

You don't have insurance.

No.

The yoga mom turns to the girl with the red backpack again. The girl seems embarrassed at being addressed, studying her bike's handlebars, but the yoga mom does not notice this. The *idiots* they let send their kids to school here, she says. People who can't afford insurance should ride the bus.

III

As she drives us down Wilshire, my mother is quiet and grips the steering wheel, her shoulders stressed because it is so high for her. Her brown makeup is shiny from sweat, and I resist an urge to tell her to pat it dry. Beyond her, sun flashes on the second floor of a parking garage, moving from car to car, glinting off hoods and chrome bumpers.

Where are we going? I say.

I need to pick some things up from the mall, she says, still sounding uptight as she turns to me. Is that *okay*?

A year ago, she would have pulled out a cigarette at this point, but she quit, and now she puts a knuckle to her mouth and chews at it. Tita Dina is always telling her this is not ladylike and she should stop.

I stare at the cupped hands in my lap.

Sure, I say.

We park out on a sunny garage roof. She remains quiet as we walk past the rows of hot clicking metal hoods and down the urine-smelling stairwell. On the sidewalk, she stops to put on her sunglasses. As I wait, I notice our reflection in a tinted window glass. Before the furniture display of slipcovered couches our reflection is ghostlike and faintly visible: a short Asian woman with a lanky teenager, one foot taller, standing amid people who swarm past.

She takes us down the Promenade, a crowded pedestrian street of fake cobblestones, towards one of the makeup shops she likes. Shoppers and tourists, couples and wanderers, come en masse from the opposite direction. The times I have been here with Tomas, people always step aside, even older men in suits with a girlfriend or secretary whom they reluctantly guide out of our way. But now my mother steps out of other people's paths, and I do too. We near a group of skinny college-student types. They look like engineers, nerdy, and I would not normally get out of their way. But even though the pale one in a yellow button-down shirt sees Mom, he acts as if he does not notice her, and she actually has to squeeze beside a bench to let them pass. The biggest one clips her shoulder. I freeze. I glare at them, aware of the ice pick tucked behind my wallet, but they don't even notice me.

She starts again and I hurry to catch up. In the past I might have walked a bit ahead, pretending not to be with her, but today I walk alongside.

A tall, model-like redhead attends the makeup counter, the Asian brand makeups high up on glass shelves behind her. She is very pretty and must be new—we haven't seen her before—and Mom instinctively clutches my arm and slows herself. She often did this before Oregon, whenever she saw a salesclerk she did not know, especially people who seemed fake or unfriendly or unusually attractive: people who she thought might look down on her accent. But today she immediately lets go of me. This girl wears a white doctor's coat, though she has pushed the sleeves above her knobby elbows, and as she moves around her skirt looks stylish without having cost much.

In the past, my mother might have pretended to look around the aisles, though I knew she was really getting ready to go up and talk to the salespeople, and when the time came she would look towards me in a way that indicated I was to come over, in case she needed help. She did not mind embarrassing me, because that went with the non-complaining territory of a dutiful Filipino son, even though I always reminded her I was American by complaining. Today I would not have complained, but she starts towards the counter without sending me the usual glance. As she nears, the cosmetics girl begins chatting across the aisle to a lady who works behind the pharmacy counter window.

My mother stands before the makeup counter, waiting. At this point you would expect the girl to turn away from her friend towards Mom, the customer, but she does not. The way my mother leans over the glass it is obvious she expects the girl to attend to her right away. But the girl continues talking, and not about an order or a work-type responsibility, but a date she had last night. Mom leans off the counter, checking to see if anyone has noticed her being ignored.

I remember the time at Fedco when the perfume sales-people passed her number and she got so upset. That day Tomas comforted her with a hand on her shoulder, and he took her crumpled number up to the counter so she could buy a perfume. But Tomas is not here today and it has fallen on me to help her. I approach. She glances up, but seeing it is me, she peers down through the glass again, as if deep in concentration.

I take a breath and pass her, reaching that part of the counter between the girl and her pharmacist friend.

Excuse me, I say.

The girl does not hear. The pharmacist notices me, but she gets distracted by some question the girl makes about her date that seems to require her attention, and returns to her conversation.

I call to the girl again.

This time I spoke louder than I intended. They turn to me, the girl's mouth gaping from a sentence she has not finished. The pharmacist woman seems concerned, but the girl stares at me.

What?

Some people need some help around here.

Mom nervously adjusts her purse strap, but the girl does not seem to notice her or that I am with her.

You know, I was in the middle of a sentence.

People have been waiting longer than that.

I'm sorry, I didn't realize you were in the need for makeup.

Did I say I needed makeup?

My hands have begun to shake, so I hide them in my pockets. The pharmacist disappears from her window and comes through a section in the countertop she lifts like a drawbridge. She's older than the girl, vaguely Hispanic, with too much purple eye shadow around her concerned eyes. She sets a hand on the girl's shoulder and faces me.

What's wrong? she says. It seems like she said this to me, but the girl answers her.

I don't know, she says. This kid comes up and all of a sudden starts talking like I was ignoring him. He only just got here.

It seems strange that my mother has not said anything yet, but she shifts around, and must be waiting for an opportunity to speak. A few shoppers have clustered at the end of a nearby aisle, and though they pretend to be looking at hair products, they in fact appear to be listening.

Hey, just cool it, Cathy, the woman says. Okay?

The girl scrunches her blue lips and her eyes narrow. We're not slaves, she mumbles.

Suddenly I am not sure whether Mom is fidgeting because she would like to say something but feels ignored, or because she wishes I had not said anything and wants to go, or that I would shut up. The girl glances at her, but Mom pretends to look at items in the counter.

It's not me, I finally tell the girl.

What? What do you mean *it's not me*?

I'm not the one waiting for help with makeup.

You're not waiting for makeup.

No.

So then what are you talking about?

Mom lowers her head, fingering the counter glass. I glance towards the glass door. Outside, a woman in denim overalls has a bright cluster of balloons for sale, bunched like floating grapes, purple and yellow, in the afternoon sunlight. Maybe, if my mother was not here, I would run to her.

I gesture towards Mom.

She's been waiting here to get service for a long time.

They swivel towards her and she smiles nervously at the girl, then lowers her head. Mom does not understand that by saying nothing she will give them the wrong impression, and so it is up to me to act quickly. I try to arrange the words in my mind, my throat constricting, but I have no idea what words will come out of my mouth.

You shouldn't not serve somebody just because they look different.

The pharmacist's face goes red. The girl looks surprised. She regards my mother, who still stares through the glass, then returns to me.

That's ridiculous, the girl says. That's. . . . She stops herself and turns to the pharmacist. Did you hear what he just said?

The woman squeezes her shoulder, then turns to me. Her expression tries to reassure me, though she is nervous. She calls out to my mother, who looks up from the glass as if she had not heard any of our conversation.

Ma'am.

Yes?

Are you looking for something?

Mom looks at her hands and seems to think about this. She lifts her face to the woman again, almost deferentially.

What?

Do you need some help?

Oh no, thank you, she blurts out. I'm just looking.

I am facing her because I do not want to turn back to the girl and woman, but she avoids my eyes, fixated on the counter and moving off a step or two. She forgets to pull her purse along and immediately realizes this, though she seems too embarrassed to pick it up, and pretends not to have noticed. It just sits there looking abandoned on the glass. The pharmacist studies us, then calls over to my mother.

Well if you need any help—

Okay. She waves her brown hand impatiently, as if she does not want to be bothered.

The woman studies me again. The ceiling slants at an angle now almost as if it were far away. I focus on a corner of drywall and the lumpy plaster visible beneath its thin layer of paint. I scrutinize it carefully, real carefully, trying to think of nothing else.

The pharmacist approaches. Her warm hand rests on my shoulder before I know it is coming and she must feel my shoulders tense and almost pull away.

Hey, are you okay? she says.

Though she's white, she sounds Puerto Rican or some sort of Spanish, and also like somebody's mother. It's strange I should know this, but somehow I feel certain.

I shrug.

Yeah.

You sure?

I make several rapid nods. I catch a glimpse of myself in the mirror and the image freezes in my mind: I look skinnier than I realized—almost bony—and my back is curved forward like a wishbone. My eyes jerk away. I wonder what I will look like—if I do not change the way I am—as an old man. In some ways, maybe, I already look it. I find myself staring down the counter and realize my mother has gone.

You got no business speaking for strangers and making unwarranted accusations, the girl says.

On the countertop, my fingers look pale and strange in the fluorescent light. The knuckles bitten and bony. The woman gives the girl an angry look and she bites her blue lip and walks away.

IV

I find my mother outside, just a few feet down from the storefront glass, where she cannot be seen, against the Dairy Store's brick wall. The sun warms the wall and glints off the gold-screened windows high above us, and Mom has found a slender shadow of an infant tree. She is always finding shade so her skin will not get darker. As we return to the car, she clutches at her purse strap, shifting it to a more comfortable position.

In the parked car she is quiet and I do not say anything, my hands cupped in my lap, and we sit in the still car, hoods popping and clicking around us. She has her key chain in her hand with the little black leather shoe the tow truck guy gave her. She does not make a movement to start the car and it seems like she wants to say something. Finally she inserts the key, then hesitates again, but gives up and starts the car.

She glances at me on Twentieth. Beneath us passes silvery asphalt whose cracks are patched up with dripped trails of black tar. The tall palm trees are so emaciated they cast thin shadows that dissolve on the street.

Do you want some frozen yogurt? she suddenly says.

I look at her.

I thought we were eating with Aunt Jessica.

We have time.

Wouldn't it spoil our appetite?

My mother has always insisted we be hungry at the meals other people buy for us, usually Aunt Jessica or my Tita Dina.

You can have an appetizer.

I shrug.

Sure.

We don't have to if you don't want to, Gabe, she says, sounding hurt. She has not looked at me but just peers over the steering wheel. She eases to a stop sign, and waits for a yellow Volkswagen Bug to pass. She used to own one when she first came to America, back when she was an emergency room receptionist and worked with some Filipino girls who all hoped to become American. They envied her her American husband, and I think most of them have married and stayed. She knows how much I love chocolate sundaes.

No, let's go.

We park a block off Montana and cross the street to avoid Aunt Jessica's store so she will not see us.

Normally she would give me money and I would buy us the ice cream, but she goes to the counter while I wait at a white plastic table, then returns with our food. Even though we are inside, it is a patio table, a canvas sun umbrella sprouting from its middle, the walls around us painted like a tropical landscape. I picked a middle table because I know she likes to sit in cafés among people, though she never talks to them. She bought a nonfat frozen yogurt for herself and a chocolate sundae with nuts and extra whipped cream for me and I eat it all and scrape the last melted bits up against the paper side and lick my spoon clean as she watches. We wait for our dinner appointment with Aunt Jessica, pretending to watch the shoppers pass outside, though at times I can feel her regarding me.

I stare at the paper cup on the table before me. Finally she reaches out and touches my cheek with her warm fingers.

Oh, Gabrielito, she says.

The plastic spoon lies in the empty container, its handle leans against the paper rim. Outside somebody passes the window; their shadow flickers across the glass and over our table and on her arms and face.

She removes her warm hand from my face and looks out the window. Her jaw trembles like an old woman's. She still wears her wedding ring.

It looks so different.

What?

All the people, she says. This street was always so empty a few years ago. Your Aunt Jessica always complained about not having restaurants nearby. Now she complains about all the strange people, even though she gets more customers.

I nod.

You want to sit outside?

Do you?

It's sunnier now.

Sure.

We find some benches in the sunlight. I can see people walking past and shoppers coming out of the Aero Theater and just next door to us some little wooden tables and black chairs set out on the sidewalk in front of the café, where people sit drinking their iced mochas in plastic cups. They all seem young and beautiful. Even the ones in jeans and T-shirts seem stylish and well dressed. I wonder how they can do this. Maybe it is the way they sit—the way the men cross their legs at the knees and delicately finger their cups. Then I notice that a few people have on expensive glasses despite their casual clothes. At the nearest table a man sits with his legs crossed this way. It is the girl's way, but he seems stylish and sits with a thin girl who could be a model and has a Rottweiler sitting at her boots. Looking closer, I see that she is probably a bit too old to be a model, though she is tall and girlish.

I try crossing my legs his way, though soon it hurts my knee and I uncross it again.

The woman catches me glancing at her and smiles, and I look down.

Tomas has always made fun of Rottweilers, but this one seems friendly and comes over. Without looking at the owners, I reach over and scratch it behind the ear.

He likes you, the man says.

The woman agrees.

I do not know what to say to this and just keep petting the dog. So they will not think I am ignoring them I lean closer to it and put my ear against it and feel the warm fur and pet him and talk to him. The woman leans over and begins talking to Mom, and though Mom seems nervous and cool towards her at first, after a while they start laughing over something. It turns out she is older than I thought because her son goes to Saint Dominic's. He is a few grades below me—I don't know him—but still, she doesn't look like she could be over twenty-five, though I guess she must be. Actually, she has lines at her mouth and eyes when she smiles, which is often, and faint blue veins on her hands. At first I do not pay attention to what my mother and the woman are saying, but only watch the way the man seems to be able to be a part of this conversation without saying anything. He has a slight relaxed smile and cups his fingers beneath his chin, nodding attentively but calmly. I try this look out in my mind, though I am shy to do it in front of him. It is something I will try later. I do try the attentive look in his eyes—watching the women closely—and start to notice what the woman is telling my mother. She says she has a car pool going—a few mothers—and asks her if she would like to join them. Mom hesitates for a moment, no doubt thinking about the rusty little Tercel, since these are the sort of people who drive Land Cruisers, and she says maybe. She will have to think about it. The woman gives my mother her number and sets her finger on her hand and after a while they say goodbye and I let the dog pull away from my cheek, patting him softly, and they leave. Mom watches them. When the woman touched my mother I could tell it made her stiffen, but now she looks at the woman for a long time. For three years she has picked me up herself, even though it meant working strange hours at the shoe department, because she did not know anybody else's mother.

I try watching people at the tables without being too obvious. They appear comfortable and talkative, though I notice a few people sitting alone. They seem at ease and look like everybody else, and peer around and observe each other. One girl, who is pretty, looks at a couple and they catch her doing this, and instead of smiling at them or even just nodding, she lowers her eyes. But she does not seem bothered about it. Not at all.

When I turn back to Mom I notice she has been watching her too, though sensing me, she immediately looks down again. Her expression stays in my mind. It is hard to figure out. Something about it bothers me, and as I think about it her face has already become a memory, and then it occurs to me—I know it is strange to think this—that what I had seen was a look of longing.

Chapter four

I

I want to tell him about Oregon—about how hard it has been on our mother, so maybe he will treat her better—but I cannot get myself to do it. He stays out many nights a week, not bothering to tell her he will not need dinner. Sometimes he brings over girlfriends, even though our mother is religious and it bothers her that they are unmarried. He does nothing around the house and leaves messes in the kitchen—plates and leftovers he does not bother to put away—which I clean up so our mother will not come home and find them there and know he did not bother. He has always stored stolen stereos in the house, but now he has them piled in the living room in plain sight. The other day Aunt Jessica came over. Mom was worried what she would think, I could tell, and veered her into the kitchen, even though it meant having her sit on an uncomfortable barstool.

Aunt Jessica went to the bathroom, though, which took her through the living room, and a few minutes later she called Mom in. My aunt was standing there looking at the stereos stacked against the wall, beneath the television set and against the bookshelves.

What are those? she said.

Mom scratched her elbow, uncomfortably. Stereos.

I can see that, Aunt Jessica said. I meant what are they doing here.

They're being stored.

Are these Tomas's?

Mom looked aside. Yes.

Aunt Jessica nodded, her lips puckered.

He buys them for cheap and sells them, Mom added quickly.

From where.

Where?

Yes, *where.*

Mom thought a moment.

He knows a boy who works in a warehouse, a discount warehouse.

So they're new.

Mom hesitated. Yes. New.

Aunt Jessica frowned. Then why aren't they in boxes?

You could see our mother's face drop, but she recovered herself and made up some answer about tax breaks. This was a lie. She had asked Tomas about the boxes and gotten only bullshit answers. My aunt did not look like she believed her, but she left Mom alone about it, for now, and they returned to the kitchen.

II

Father Ryan comes to a party at my Tita Dina's house. He always gets invited by my aunt, who likes priests, because he lived in the Philippines for so long. Tita always puts out Filipino dishes brunch-style in the kitchen along with

Chinese food from Madame Wu's, and people serve themselves, then make their way to the dining room. They always make sure Father Ryan sits at the dining table next to Tita Dina, a special place. This time some of my mother's cousins are in town from San Jose and sit there and my mother does too. I can see and hear all of them talking, from the family room, where I sit before a silent TV that plays the Bulls game.

My mother often gets cheerful at the parties on a glass of wine. Maybe she feels lonely most of the time and that is why she especially enjoys her cousins' company. Yesterday they went to Disneyland with her cousin's little daughter Veronica and came back with bags of T-shirts to bring home to my cousins and little trinkets and souvenirs. The girl had taken a liking to Mom, even persuading her to go on Space Mountain with her. She used her mother's money to buy Mom a little Mickey Mouse sweatshirt which I know Mom will not wear, but I can tell she likes it because she showed it off to people as though it were a piece of jewelry. She has it at the table as she tells Father Ryan about the rides they went on and the fun they had.

He smiles and nods attentively in his Filipino way.

Have you ever been on Pirates of the Caribbean, Father Ryan?

Oh, no, he laughs, gently.

For some reason all the Filipinas at the table find his reaction funny and start laughing. Soon, though, my mother's cousin Tai Pei starts talking about her son who works in Silicon Valley, how he bought a new Mercedes and plans on building a guest cottage behind his house for her to live in in her old age. Somehow the conversation gets on to all their children, the colleges they go to, and their jobs. I pretend not to listen. Mom quietly fingers her empty wine-glass, her head slightly lowered. Father Ryan notices this. Earlier Tomas had come in wearing a sleeveless undershirt that showed off his tattoos and got food from the kitchen and ate in a corner without smiling at anyone. I could tell from his bloodshot eyes that he was stoned. Father Ryan noticed this too.

My brother sat there staring at his plate, occasionally picking at food, scraping his paper plate with his knife and licking it clean. My cousin Matt came in then, late, with his girlfriend, who is some Jewish girl who went to Westward and now goes to Berkeley. Matt is a little older, twenty-five, and teaches English. Though Matt is half Filipino like us, he dresses like the rich white kids he went to school with. I remember in the eighties he wore a pink Polo shirt, though now he is in a fashionable dark brown suede leather coat with seventies style lapels and huge drooping buttons, Doc Martens, and black pants. His school was only a mile away from ours. It is strange how differently we turned out. My mother says he goes to temple on Saturdays with her family and attends classes on Jewish mysticism, which bothers his mother, who buys him books by Thomas Merton on Catholic meditation. Tita also sends money to some Indian nuns on a reservation in New Mexico, to pray for his soul. They got their food from the buffet in the kitchen and on their way to the dining room passed Tomas. Matt paused a second, glancing down at my brother, and Tomas nodded up, coolly, and I could tell that Matt knew he was stoned. Matt was surprised, but didn't want to alienate my brother, and so tried to hide his reaction. The girlfriend was trying not to appear too curious about my brother, or afraid, and used my cousin, whom she stood behind, as a shield between them. She cupped his arm.

How's it going, Tomas? Matt said.

My brother looked at Matt like this was a farce. They both knew Matt did not like the way my brother behaved, so why pretend. Matt had always come over to our house to tutor him, though that stopped when he went off to college back east. The same falling-off happened with me. For some reason we did not pick up with the tutoring after he returned.

Yeah, cool, man, Tomas said, looking down at his plate again.

Matt and his girlfriend traded glances (as if to say, *What's he on?*) but said nothing, then Matt went into the dining room and they ate with the Filipinos.

III

Now, through Tita Dina's French doors, I notice Tomas sitting on the diving board, the sun on his tank top brilliantly white and almost blinding, as he stares down into the pool. The reflection off the water moves over his face and chest like thin little arms of lightning. I return to the ball game. When I look out again my brother has disappeared. Mom has been glancing outside anxiously all afternoon, and I figure I should go and check up on him. I find him around the side of the house with Veronica, Mom's little niece. He is showing her the Colt he likes to carry around and has the barrel open and shows her how you can look through an empty chamber and see sky through the other end. He also has a few bullets on the concrete and lets her handle one. She looks up at me, her expression turning from excitement to worry, and though I let my shadow fall across his legs, he pretends he does not see me. She sets the bullet down on an empty plastic lawn chair, the kind you can stack, its surface lightly filmed over with soot from smoggy dew that has dried. Tomas asks her if she wants to hold the Colt, and she glances at me, then shakes her head. Then she senses his annoyance and takes it into her little hand.

Do you think you should be doing that? I say to him.

He does not even look up.

I go back to my Bulls game. Later, much later, I hear some sort of commotion and notice Veronica's mother kneeling over her, asking angry questions, and the girl avoids her eyes and only reluctantly nods. The mother keeps staring through the French windows at Tomas, who sits in the sunlight, indifferent, slouched on the end of a reclining lawn chair.

By six, everyone has left but us. Empty chairs sit on the backyard grass and on the wooden gazebo and on the concrete by the pool. Despite the vines and flowers my aunt planted on the backyard's rear wooden fence to make it look tranquil, I hear faint traffic coming from the other side. I am picking up plates and taking them into the kitchen where Tita washes dishes, tossing the paper ones the kids had to use into a trash bag. When Tita goes upstairs to answer a phone call, Mom walks up to my brother.

What the hell do you think you were doing out there, mister? she says. Her hands on her hips. She is angry, not merely trying to *look* angry the way she usually does with Tomas when she wants him to take her seriously.

My brother's eyes are not as bloodshot as they have been, and he seems a little surprised and off guard as he looks up at her from his chair.

What you so mad about?

I think you know, Tomas.

I can't read your mind.

Your Tita Nene was very disappointed in you.

Who the fuck is she?

Your *Tita Nene*? Don't try telling me you don't know your Tita Nene, Tomas.

She's Veronica's mom, I tell him.

He looks at me, annoyed. Shut up, Junior.

He seems in no mood for joking so I back off. He turns to Mom. Your relative gets all excited real easy doesn't she? he says.

I'm not joking, Tomas.

I didn't do anything.

She turns towards the pool and the light off the house's white stucco wall illuminates her face, and she seems to hold her words, then turns back to him. Let me see the gun.

What?

Let me see the gun.

He shrugs as if he does not care, though it is obvious he does. He turns to me. I don't know what she's talking about. Do you, Junior?

I ignore him.

He seems to believe she will drop this and walk inside, but she does not move. She scratches her elbow the way she does when nervous, though now she is only angry.

How could you do this to me? Her eyes are wide and almost watery.

Tomas shifts uncertainly. Sorry, he says.

She looks away. Her jaw almost trembling.

He leans forward, as though about to put a hand on her shoulder—something he used to do when he was younger. He does not, though.

How humiliating, our mother says. She keeps her eyes away from his. I can't believe you would do this to me.

He glances at me, panicked for help, but finding nothing, he turns back to her again.

Jesus, Mom, he says. I said I'm sorry.

IV

A week later we get the first phone call. At least it is the first phone call I know of. If the yoga mom has talked to our mother before, I have not heard about it. I tell the woman my mother is not home, which is true, and say I will tell her she called. I do not, and hope maybe the yoga mom will drop it, but in the evening Tomas answers the phone, and even listening from the other room, I can tell he is speaking to her, and he sounds impatient and annoyed and angry. He returns to the kitchen.

Jesus, he says.

What?

That bitch is pissed at Mom.

It seems that the yoga mom wants to take her Land Cruiser in to get repaired. She already took it to the dealer and got an estimate. My brother looks too worked up to sit down. He is so mad at her he has forgotten to be nasty to me.

It was just a little scratch, I say. Her truck was so big the Tercel could barely do any damage.

She said it was going to be eight hundred dollars.

That's bullshit, I say.

He shakes his head.

I tell him how she humiliated our mother in front of school, before most of the kids and many of their carpooling parents.

What do you think we should do? he says. It is rare that he would ask me such a question.

If she calls again let's tell her Mom's not home.

He nods absently, deep in thought.

The next day she calls and Mom is home but I tell the woman she is not. The woman sounds like she does not believe me.

Did you give your mother my message? she says.

I wrote it down.

Well I want you to *tell* it to her this time, she says. She did not say *please* but I tell her I will and hope she will give up. But she calls again two hours later and I will not answer the phone so Tomas goes over and tells her he wrote down the message *and stop calling us if you're going to use a rude tone of voice* and he hangs up on her. The phone rings again and he picks it up without listening to the receiver and drops it into the cradle again. The plastic clicks and rattles. After that we do not answer it and tell our mother not to answer it.

Why? she says.

It's Maria, he says.

Did you two get into a fight again?

That's right.

But the next evening she answers the phone and we listen to her whole conversation. Our mother is all quiet, nodding obediently again. It is as if she were in the same room with the yoga mom. Then she tells the woman she does not have insurance. Some time goes by. I can tell by the look on her face that she is getting chewed out.

You should make her get another estimate, Tomas says to Mom later. Eight hundred bucks is outrageous. It's a complete rip-off.

I could have given our mother some advice or told the woman a few things but I sit in the corner very still with my arms crossed. When the yoga mom calls back, Tomas answers and tells her eight hundred dollars is too much and that he would be happy to take it someplace where he knows people and can get a deal. The woman tells him she wants to get it done by a reputable dealer, and anyway she does not want anyone else driving her car.

But they're ripping you off, he says. Look. You might be used to getting ripped off and not care, but some people can't afford not to shop around.

He listens to her say something more.

Fucking bitch, he says, and hangs up.

Mom looks upset.

Did you have to say that, Tomas?

What?

Did you have to call her by those words?

You're saying you want me to be nice to her?

Mom does not answer him, clearly flustered.

Where you gonna get eight hundred dollars? he says. *I'll* be the one who will have to pay.

No, Tomas.

And you don't even want to let me bargain the price down.

I told you. I won't let you pay.

It's not the money, he says. It's the *principle*. And anyway where are you going to get the money?

I'll find a way.

You'll find a way.

Listen, Tomas, I don't want you being rude again.

The next time the phone rings Tomas tries to get it out of her hand, but she will not let him. He storms out of the room and goes outside. He works the dogs in the dark for another hour and we can hear him out there, the barks and clattering cage and the sound of them hitting my brother and slamming him against the wooden fence.

After that Tomas is mad at her and does not talk to her and is even worse about not picking things up around the house. He has been nicer to us in general ever since the incident with Veronica. I think this has affected Mom. She even hoped, probably stupidly, that she could get him to work again and to study his way back into Saint Dominic's. But in a moment that all changed.

And at school, now, I will see the yoga mom's son, Ben, in assembly. He sits at the other side of the auditorium, right up front by the speaker, and I cannot tell if he knows anything about what his mother is doing. A couple of times he catches me looking at him, but I do not get the sense he knows I am angry. Once in the crowded hallway between periods he even says hello and I decide he cannot know anything but I feel like hurting him anyway, and have to take long walks to calm down.

We thought maybe we had heard the last of his mother, but then she comes up to Mom's car in front of the whole school again. Ben stands there, avoiding my eyes, pretending he does not know what is happening. Maybe he believes this is grown-up business and does not involve him and me. My mother tries to get the yoga mom to hold off on the payment and the woman tells her she has already made an appointment with the dealer and if she doesn't get the money she will call the authorities and tell them our mother does not have insurance. I really want to say something to this woman, but for some reason I do not. Within a week, Mom begins looking for an extra night job, though she tells me not to let my brother find out.

V

Yesterday I found a letter from Uncle Betino with post stamps from Manila. It was on my mother's makeup drawer and I could tell from its crinkles that she had read it many times.

Dear Ika,

I was heartened to discuss with you that you wish finally to send your son(s) to Manila, as I have been encouraging you to do for some time. Of course I was disturbed to hear that Gabe has lost his admission to Westward due to falling grades, but perhaps he needs the discipline of a Filipino Catholic school and another culture away from the unfortunate influences he now is experiencing in Los Angeles. Immediately I have called Father Reyoso who is well acquainted with the fathers at Ateneo to see about their application. Unfortunately, due to the lateness of this inquiry it will not be possible to send Gabe there now. It may be possible to send him in the spring if he can keep his grades from falling further and out of disciplinary problems, as you have been worrying he will encounter lately.

In fact, I do not think that Tomas could gain admittance to attend even in the spring. There are of course other schools we can look into, and I will make inquiries through Father Reyoso, but I think it will perhaps be best if I secure for him a tutor and keep him at Forbes Park under my personal supervision. If it will be possible to discipline him myself, I will. With Gabe I think it may still be possible to instill in him some of the Asian virtues of our family heritage, of discipline and education and respect for elders and history, as well as some of the European virtues of our Spanish and German heritage, of culture and learning imbued to

our mother from the German nuns at Saint Scholastica. However,
with Tomas, I fear you have waited too long and not listened to
me, and that it is too late. He has become a gangster and is in my
mind no longer a Filipino or a Laurel.

It is a shame. I recall when he last came to visit us he
seemed a sweet well-behaved boy, if a little shy, though after an
initial timidity he came to enjoy playing with the Filipino children
and especially took a liking to the animals on the farm such as a
particular carabao he named Emilio and became upset when he
was told he could not bring it home. Your Tita Effre gave him a
wooden water buffalo to console him but he smashed it against
a wall. I was surprised, but it has since occurred to me that
sometimes the quiet ones have the more mysterious anxieties
inside that are difficult for the rest of us to understand. If he will
sign a promise to obey me, I will have him in the house.
Otherwise, I would like to separate him from his younger brother
and focus on Gabe.

I will call you when I get further word from Father Reyoso on
the status of his inquiries. In the meantime your youngest son
will have a place in our prayers.

Your brother
Betino

VI

He comes to me when I am out back playing with Greta,
scratching her behind the ear and getting ready to take her
for a walk.

Come on, he says.

I am kneeling by her, the warmth of her fur coming
through my jeans, and he stands high above me. His face is
silhouetted by the blue sky. Behind him a skywriter has left a

trail of white clouds, the ghostlike etchings of blurred words I can no longer understand.

Where?

What do you mean where? Don't you worry about that.

I do not move.

Is it to train a dog?

He looks annoyed. The muscles along his forearms tense.

No, it's not to train a dog. Now get your ass in gear, Junior.

I shake my head, one bony elbow supporting my weight on my knee.

I'm not going.

I can feel him wanting to take a step forward. Greta senses this too and her body tenses beside me. Tomas holds back, not wanting to hit me in front of one of the dogs. They are loyal dogs and dependable, and though they are really his dogs, you could never know what would happen if two brothers started fighting. He knows that I know this and he looks away a moment, then turns back again.

I don't care what you want to do. You still owe me for Buster.

Greta's chest heaves and I can feel her rapid breathing.

The back door rattles in its aluminum frame and both of us turn and see our mother come out onto the porch and shade her eyes. She wears a pink little tailored jacket she designed and cut herself. She must see us, but for some reason turns around and goes back inside. Then I can see her movements through the window, only the shape of her walking behind the screen, and I wonder if she is dusting the pane or watching us.

Greta rubs the side of her head into the back of my hand, wanting me to scratch her.

Maybe you shouldn't keep those stereos out where Mom can see them.

She doesn't know.

I wouldn't be so sure.

He ignores me and goes over to the cage and the dogs clamber excitedly against the wire and he opens the door—keeping them back with his shoe—and calls to Greta. She hesitates beside me but leaves my side and enters through the door. He snaps the cage door shut and the links clatter and settle and he comes over and hits me in the face. The dogs circle and bark and throw themselves against the chain link and it rattles and ripples and then they fall back to the concrete ground.

In the car I pretend not to feel any pain. I taste the salty blood in my mouth and my tongue traces the folds of flesh that have torn against my teeth. We drive silently, past where the Taquería on Bundy is now a Starbucks and down Santa Monica westward by the car dealers where it is all bright sidewalks and concrete with only a few anemic sapling trees and I can see weeds growing from enormous cracks in the sidewalks here, even from my window. Though it was sunny at our house, we hit the marine-layer overcast that creeps in west of Twentieth Street.

He glances over at me, but I ignore him.

Don't look so hurt, Junior, you'll get over it.

I'm not hurt.

Sure.

The wind whistles through my window at the crack between the glass and ceiling.

Maybe afterwards we'll get some Häagen-Dazs, he says after a while.

I do not answer. We used to go for Häagen-Dazs on the

corner of Vincente and Barrington, and it was so popular and crowded then that you had to get in line and hustle to make sure the ice cream boy or girl saw you. The tables would be full and all the people in the warm night drifting outside and licking their cones. Still Mom would stand there shivering and hugging herself against the wind that to us was not cold. Tomas and I would hover around the inside café tables like vultures, forcing people to leave. That Häagen-Dazs is not there anymore, only a Coffee Bean where all the young movie-industry types sip their blended mochas.

He flips the radio on, then tries to thump his hand against the dashboard to the beat, then turns it off and faces me again. He sets his elbow on the top of the rolled-down window glass.

Junior's angry, he says.

I ignore him.

Look, if you're going to be a deaf-mute then maybe you shouldn't sit up in front. Front-seat passengers don't get to be boring.

I'm not deaf.

That's what it sounds like to me.

Just because someone is being mute doesn't necessarily mean they're deaf.

Whatever.

Well don't go saying things like that if you're going to be wrong and inaccurate.

We pass San Vincente on Seventh and head down the hill into Rustic Canyon. Here fog has crept into the valley floor and you can see the red taillights glowing before us. A rig coming up from the PCH nears, its bone white head-lights glowing and misted before and above us, like twin suns obscured by fog, then it shudders past.

You know you embarrass Mom.

He pauses a moment. I doubt that, Junior, he says. You're the one who's ugly.

I keep quiet. I can feel what I said bothering him, though he does not want me to know this.

I don't embarrass Mom, he finally says.

Okay, whatever you want to believe.

He looks at me.

So?

So what.

Am I gonna have to beat the fuck out of you or are you going to tell me what you mean.

It's the way you dress, and behave at parties.

He laughs. That's all you mean.

It's enough.

He ignores me as we pull behind the line of cars at the PCH traffic light, and even across the wide highway I can faintly make out the misted ocean and empty beach. The sand appears hard and damp, still bearing the furrows from the tractors that rake litter and glass from it each morning. A newly seeded farm field covered by a windstorm's drifting sand.

We head up into the Palisades. On the far canyon wall you can see the four-story villa with its pink sides, sunny above the creeping mist.

You know, you're the one to talk, Junior.

What do you mean?

He waits a moment, gripping his steering wheel casually. I don't know. Just a thought.

No. What?

He takes a breath and you can hear the in-suck of air entering his throat.

I know you think you're the nice son and everything.

I never said I think that.

He gives me a look. The way I remember it, you were always crying in restaurants. You'd throw tantrums before the first day of school and she had to bring you in herself. It was embarrassing. You were always getting beat up. Man, was she worried about you.

He faces forward, waiting for me to say something. I don't.

She couldn't take you nowhere. If we went to a party at a relative's house, she could never stay long—no matter how much fun she was having—because someone would find you hiding in some closet, or you'd have walked off down the street and some uncle would have to go looking for you. I know for a fact she was embarrassed. But she was afraid some bully would've gotten to you so she'd make an uncle look for you. Sometimes a whole group of them would go, like a search party.

I look at my fingers. You wouldn't know that, I say.

Yeah I know.

Bullshit.

He turns to me. You want me to spell it out, Junior? He stops, regarding me, then shakes his head and looks forward again. He seems to have decided to stop speaking, but then changes his mind.

I heard her saying it once.

Okay, I interrupt.

I *heard* her saying it once. Apologizing to Tito Bentong for the way you ran off and made everyone look after you all over the neighborhood. She was practically crying. A bunch of her cousins were there from the Philippines, and a classmate from Santo Tomas. She hadn't seen them in years.

Mom had made a dress just for the occasion, brought a pot of Lola's paella. You'd found your way into a neighbor's backyard and hid in the bushes. The neighbor—this old dude—had found you and called the police and it took a long time before they got you to us. By the time people could eat, everything was cold. We had to leave before it was even served. Then Mom had to take us through a McDonald's drive-through because you said you were hungry. We ate in the car.

He pauses, his brows furrowed in thought. It reminds me of the way he used to look whenever he was doing math. The funny thing is, Gabe, you were mute most of the time, and everyone thought you were so well behaved, but at home you'd have these tantrums in front of her. She'd give you whatever you wanted. I guess you somehow felt that she would. You *knew* it. Suddenly, he stares at me. I never see you doing that anymore, though, Junior, he says, almost as though this is something to be sad about.

We drive down into Rustic Canyon. Dusty sunlight flickers through the ropy leaves of overhanging eucalyptus trees, and I catch glimpses of houses through the wooded roadside. The road narrows and winds. As we enter the fog again, he turns on his windshield wipers.

We are quiet. I feel his eyes on me, but he does not say anything. After a while he studies me again.

Are you going to cry?

No.

Man, I can't take you anywhere.

We enter the private drive, which is a dirt road through a forest. Looking ahead, I glimpse a modern house, made of glass and white concrete, in a sunny clearing. There are no cars in the driveway, but he parks behind some trees short of the front lawn. He kills the motor. I wait for him to get out but he just sits there.

So are you coming in or do you want me to pick up some tissues and bring them back for you?

I ignore him and open my door and step onto the long, crispy grass, slamming the door behind me. It was stupid to make a loud sound but Tomas does not get mad. He just grins at me. Up near the house the grass becomes well cut—a lawn—and the driveway becomes paved. The house seems to be built half in the sunny clearing, half around the edge of the woods. I hear him shutting his car door softly and his footsteps crunching the coarse wild grass as he nears.

I am nervous now and start worrying about how Mom would feel if we got caught.

I'm not going, I suddenly tell him.

Why?

I'm just not.

An evil-looking smile comes across his lips. You don't even know whose house this is, Junior.

A gentle breeze smelling faintly of the ocean runs across my neck, slips down my shirt back. *Whose* house is it then?

Why should I tell *you*? It's not like you care.

Care about what?

He goes to the Explorer and opens the rear and reaches inside. He pulls out a tire iron and slaps it against his palm, then grips it.

Okay. You know that yoga mother who keeps nagging Mom about that stupid dent in her car?

You mean Ben Feinstein's mom?

He nods towards the carport tucked between the house

and garage, which I had not noticed before. In it is parked the black Land Cruiser. Its tinted windows are almost as black as the paint.

He comes over and stands right next to me. So close his shoulder touches my own. That's the truck that bitch humiliated Mom in front of school about, right?

The sun throbs hot against my temples.

That pissed you off, didn't it?

I nod.

I could tell, Junior. I could really tell.

He watches wind blow through the prickly red chaparral treetops, high above, like warm breath moving over thorns. His shoulder against my shoulder bone feels warm and strangely gentle.

Are you game? he says.

Yeah.

We crunch through the long grass and make it onto the lawn, soft and lumpy under our feet—the kind of pre-grown grass people pay gardeners to roll on. It smells of fertilizer, and I can see the edges of the squares they rolled out. The car sits covered by a trellis between the garage and house, sunlight coming through the grapevines above and lighting it in patches. Tomas comes up to the car and peers inside.

Alarm's on, he says.

I ask for the tire iron and he holds it out and I take it in my hand and my blood moves in my fingers against it and it feels warm and heavy and hard.

He goes up to the rear bumper. There is a scrape on the paint and the rubber is scuffed. Tomas reaches out with his shoe and taps it softly. The dent is so small nobody would notice unless it was pointed out, but she still had to call our mother and demand from her money that would take her two weeks of work to earn.

I step towards the car.

Hey, what are you guys doing here? a small voice says.

We turn. Ben Feinstein stands in the doorway that leads to the house. The kitchen behind him is huge and I can make out a far kitchen table and a counter of butcher-block wood lit by an unseen skylight. Above it hang shiny copper pots and pans.

Tomas approaches him.

Hey, Ben, he says, smiling and extending his hand.

Ben looks at it and hesitates. Tomas was never nice to him at school, but Ben finally shakes Tomas's hand, then smiles at him. He wears a red polo vest that people make fun of but which his mother likes.

We came to pay your mom for the damage our mom did to her car. Is she around?

Ben looks over his shoulder but tells us she is not. He seems happy to hear this explanation for why we are here.

That's too bad, Tomas says, pretending to sound disappointed. Hey, would it be all right if we paid *you*?

Me? Ben's hands are shoved in his pockets.

Tomas turns to me. Junior, you got my wallet?

It takes me a second to figure out what he wants.

No, I say.

Shit. I think I left it in the car.

He turns back to Ben. We're parked at the end of the drive. Come on back and we'll give it to you.

Ben hesitates but nods. We begin walking towards the woods. Above the treetops emerges a white mission-style church with an ornate bell tower.

Hey, that's a nice vest you got there.

Thanks.

Polo?

Ben nods.

Where'd you get it?

Israel.

You had to go all the way over there to get a Polo vest?

No, my grandma got it for me. She buys me presents every time we go there.

Is it true all the men over there have to join the military and learn martial arts and shit?

Yeah.

I heard in the Mossad they learn jujitsu by doing flips on concrete. You know anything about that?

Ben hesitates but finally tells my brother he has not heard of that. Whenever he looks up at my brother, the sun captures his face and makes him squint, but his eyes remain riveted on Tomas. I've fallen back, and have to take a couple steps forward to try and read my brother's expression and figure out what he is up to.

As we walk onto the longer grass Tomas senses some hesitation in me because he gives me a look—as if to say *See this*—and then turns to Ben, who follows close behind him.

Listen. Sorry about the way our mom's so late with the money, he says.

That's okay.

Yeah, but it must be really annoying.

Ben shrugs, walking with his head down.

Sometimes she can be a real space cadet, Tomas says.

Again, Ben does not say anything.

Like the way she hit your mother's car. I mean they were only going a couple miles an hour. Tomas shakes his head. You know how clueless old oriental ladies like her can get.

Yeah, Ben says, chuckling, happy to be included in a conversation with him.

And the way she talks. Tomas shakes his head even more now. You ever talked to her, Ben?

I know what you mean, he says eagerly.

We walk in silence.

My brother looks at me now to make sure I've been listening. The hair on the back of my neck has pricked like needles, and the air is motionless. We get to the car.

Hey, Ben, I'm gonna look in the front seat, Tomas says. Can you take a look in back?

Ben turns towards the backseat window to peer inside, obviously doing it to please him. He has to lean close because the glass is tinted, and I can see his faint, squinting reflection as my brother gives me a look. But I am already coming up behind him and grab his hair and shove his face into the glass. There is a loud thuck as if no skin separates the glass and bone. Ben tries to struggle free and nearly pushes me off balance, so I thump his forehead into the glass again. It hits harder than I intended, and I hesitate, but he nearly gets free and pokes my eye in the process. It is all I can do to pin his lower back with my hip, shoving him against the door handle. Tomas tells me to hold him and I manage to get his arms wrapped around the small of his back. As my brother punches his stomach I can feel the blows through his back and his body slouching as his legs give way. I let him fall to the ground.

Pick him up, Tomas tells me.

I grab him by the shoulders and Ben doesn't resist. He even pushes up to help me.

My brother asks me if I have my ice pick and tells me to set it against him. The silver end indents easily against his soft cheek, jitters in my fingers. Most of his head is turned away from us but I can feel in his shoulders that he is crying.

Tomas leans close to his ear. That was some mean shit you said about our mother.

I can feel Ben's heartbeat through his warm damp clothing, where I grip his elbows. He tries to keep still, though he has a hard time calming his rapid breathing.

I'm sorry.

It wasn't me you insulted.

I'm sorry to your mom.

My brother breathes in his ear. She's poor as shit. And your mother wants eight hundred dollars.

I'm sorry.

For a fucking little scratch.

I'm sorry.

I piss on your mother. Puta.

Tomas taps Ben's cheek beside the ice pick and Ben's body jerks.

You got eight hundred dollars inside?

Ben's eyes widen. No.

You got an awfully expensive wardrobe. You got adult spending habits.

My parents buy the stuff for me. I don't get it myself.

His shirt is really damp now, slippery against my fingers. He glances at me, pleadingly, then turns away again. He is actually afraid of me. Maybe he worries that he gave the impression that he does not think of me as being tough like my brother. I look over at Tomas. He catches my eye and seems pleased with me. I turn to concentrate on Ben so it will not look like I am avoiding Tomas's gaze. A couple of times in the past I have been with a small group of people when someone said a few smart-aleck things about me and

Ben laughed even though I was older. But now he is respectful, his head bowed.

And though my stomach wrenches, I feel a rush not of anxiety but of confidence. In a scary way I realize I like it. Strangely, that only makes my stomach worse.

Tomas holds out the tire iron and I hesitate but take it. By the time I have finished swinging it across Ben's legs and arms his shirt is torn and damp. My blood is hot and beating in my hand where I grip the tire iron, and I drop it.

My brother gently cups the back of Ben's neck, almost stroking it.

If you tell anybody about this we will come by and beat up your mother.

The bottom of Ben's hair presses into his collar as he nods.

You understand?

Okay.

No, you *really* understand?

Yes.

Tomas smoothes Ben's hair. Listen to me. When people ask you who did this, and you are dying to talk, I want you to remember this conversation. I want you to remember the things you said about our mother and how much we hate you for it. And I want you to imagine all the things we could do to your mom.

VII

We drive up the curving misted roads, the sun a yellow blur, and come out onto Sunset.

Tomas studies me. We have caught late afternoon traffic and creep behind a bottleneck of cars that moves toward a

Pacific Palisades stoplight. To the southwest, the sun is cradled low in some shaggy palm tops, high above a shimmering red roof. Dying light bleeds across the houses of the far canyon wall.

Don't look so deflated, Junior.

I'm not deflated.

He looks forward again and seems to ponder this. He nods. He sets his hand on me and I tense because he has never done it this way before, but the gesture feels somehow familiar. Then it dawns on me that this is probably something that my father used to do to both of us.

Good, he says.

After a while he turns onto Allenford and we start to head south. I ask him where we are going.

How's your appetite?

Actually I have none, but I do not want to admit this.

It's strong, I say.

Acknowledgements

I would like to thank my parents, Thomas and Azucena, and sister, Carla, and wife, Gwen, for their love and support. My Varvaro cousins for their stories and humor and information about attack dogs. Thanks also to Noah Lukeman, Tom Bissell, and Amy Cherry for believing in me and helping the book along. And for their fine readings of the manuscript: Drew Bennett, Maryam Keshavarz, Michael Koch, Tom Jenks, Gwen and Carla Roley, and all those people who have seen pieces of it and offered up their comments. And for their advice and encouragement: Maureen McCoy, Lamar Herrin, Helena Viramontes, Alison Lurie, and especially Dan McCall and Stephanie Vaughn.